VAMPIRE MAGE

A Clutch Mistress Book

Janelle Peel

For my family—
those that have believed in me here
and those in heaven.
Thank you.

~Janelle

Contents

Chapter 1

Sora

Curley's sported broken neon in bright red letters over a chipped brick building with bars covering the windows. The *r* was either burnt out or broken and spelled "Culey's." Cute, I thought, pushing my way into the dimly lit interior.

After a quick scan of the patrons, I noted a dark corner with a single occupant at the opposite end of the bar. Cracked tile greeted my Chucks as I threaded my way over between the rickety tables.

Garth Brooks played out of an old jukebox in the corner. Half the screen was lit, and I could barely make out the warbles of "Friends in Low Places." *Low* being the key word in my mind.

Easing onto a crooked stool, I placed my wallet on the only clean surface: the bar.

A portly man with a handlebar mustache shuffled over with a grunt.

"Tequila, please, Pepsi back," I mumbled, earning another grumble by way of reply.

Pulling some loose change from the pocket of my apron, I hoped to have enough to put Garth in the back of the queue, and made my way over to the jukebox. As I flipped through the selections using the worn silver knobs, the paper placards flopped beneath the scratched glass. I quickly said a prayer to the All Mother for there to be some classic rock—anything other than country.

Yes! I smiled. "Paint It Black." Making my selection, I popped in two quarters and headed back to my chair.

As the Stones finally shut down Garth, I eyed my drink. After a steadying inhale, I polished the shot in one go. Mouth watering at the taste, I quickly chased it with the glass of warm Pepsi. Ick. Gut rot stuff.

Shadows moved out of the corner of my eye. Turning my head, I caught a glimpse of blond hair and a strong jaw as my bar mate shifted his position.

Plucking my phone from the back pocket of my jeans, I squinted at the sudden bright light. 1:30 a.m. The bartender was polishing the aged oak down the way, so I raised my cup.

"A double, please."

Grabbing the bottle, he poured four fingers of gold, and went back to his task.

I stared hard at my glass, wondering where the hell I was, and who the hell I was. My days had taken on a monotony of sleep, eat, and work. It was all autopilot since Giselle took me in four months ago. I shopped at thrift stores for clothes, but that was about all I did to leave my studio apartment. A mini fridge, free Netflix, and a microwave were my stable companions. My cell was an outdated Nokia. It didn't even have data, not that I'd have a use for it.

My friend Viv owned an internet cafe, but her being human made me feel more like an imposter.

Reaching for the glass, I raised it to my lips and slowly swallowed the burn just to feel something as Mick hummed out his last tones. Switching to the warm soda to ease the fire in my throat, I debated on playing another song or heading back to my *Orange Is the New Black* binge.

A brush of air whispered against my neck, prickling my skin as the only other patron made their exit.

I stewed a bit more on things I couldn't change and checked the time: 1:45 a.m. Throwing a few bills on the bar, I gathered my things and left.

Once outside, I zipped up my hoodie and shoved my hands deep into its pockets. It was chilly for a June night in San Diego. The weatherman had forecasted a light drizzle. Looking up, I searched for the silver face of the Moon, but the marine layer was too thick. I was getting spoiled; only fifty degrees out and I was freezing. I concentrated on my footsteps for the two-mile walk home, and my vision slightly blurred while I berated myself for skipping dinner after the evening rush.

Wallowing back in my own self-pity, thoughts of my ineptitude flashed through my mind. I had everything; how could I be a magical dud? My parents had maxed out on what they could do for me, but when they could no longer deny my inability to cast even a light sphere, the Council forced them to cast me out. By that point they were so frustrated and embarrassed by what should have been a child prodigy, they didn't even accompany me to my own banishment. As I recalled the last time I had seen them at dinner before I was taken away like trash, I failed to pay attention to my surroundings.

Without warning, I was hit from my right side and thrown to the sidewalk. The world spun as my head slammed against the unforgiving concrete. I caught a glimpse of blond hair just before my world went black.

I was being shaken. Rough hands began patting down my pockets.

"What?" I mumbled groggily.

A male voice shouted in alarm, "Shit, she's waking up! Let's go!"

Slowly, I sat up to the slaps of their retreating footsteps and took in my surroundings. Only about a quarter mile from home. My fingers dug into the grass and bumped into the hard brick of my phone as I swayed to my knees. Snatching it to my chest, I thought it was absurdly comical that not even random thieves wanted the old piece of junk. Further inspection revealed my apron was a ripped mess and my wallet was missing.

Goddess, my head hurt. Reaching to the back of my skull with my free hand, I found a solid knot with the makings of a scab. Had I fallen?

I rocked back to sit on my heels, and my cell cheerily glowed, 4:30 a.m.

I ran through what I remembered: bar, tequila, time 1:45 a.m. About two missing hours. Maybe I drank too much? Staggering to my feet, I finally made it over to the sidewalk and continued home with my thoughts a scattered mess.

Ten minutes later, the light on the landing glowed like a beacon as I reached my studio. Leaning heavily on the rail, I slowly climbed the stairs. Thankfully, my keys had been safe in my inner jacket pocket.

After repeatedly missing the keyhole, I cursed myself. Had I really drunk too much and fallen over?

Eventually, I found the lock and turned the key. Fumbling the knob, I stumbled inside.

Kicking the door closed with my heel, I flicked the deadbolt and tossed my phone onto the hide-a-bed. Using the wall for support, I slowly made my way to the small bathroom and flipped on the light.

My platinum hair was stained orange from the impact with the concrete. Dull sea-green eyes stared back at me from a reflection I barely recognized. The smattering of freckles on the bridge of my nose, normally not even noticeable, stood out in stark relief. My sun-kissed tan was gone; I looked like death after a bender with a bottle of José.

Turning away in disgust, I turned the shower on as hot as I could stand and quickly shucked my clothes. Pulling the flimsy plastic curtain aside, I stepped under the spray. Oh, blessed heat. Swiftly, I soaped my locks and bits as anxiety fluttered through my belly. I just wanted to go to sleep and put the entire night behind me.

After a rough towel dry, I tugged on a tank and loose shorts before hopping into bed. Snuggling beneath my blue blanket, I flipped through my saved shows on the TV. Sleep finally arrived with the remote still clutched tightly in my hand.

I awoke to the standard sound of my Nokia tune. Blindly searching through the covers, I finally located the device once the ringing stopped. 4:30 p.m. I'd slept for nearly twelve hours. My thoughts scrambled as I tried to remember what day it was. Right, Wednesday, my night off. My phone chimed as a message scrolled across the display.

'Hey, honey! Dinner tonight at 6?' A big *G* shone next to the text—Giselle. She liked having dinner once a week. She worried about me. Her husband and daughter had passed away a year ago in a car accident.

I slowly typed back, 'I got in late last night. Raincheck for tomorrow?'

'Are you okay?'

'Fine, just a long night.'

'Let me know if you need anything. Get some rest :/'

I loved it when she used emoticons. It was sweet. 'Will do :)'

As I looked around my studio, the events of last night came rushing back. What the hell had happened?

My stomach rumbled loudly. Well, I mused, that was one problem I could solve. Getting up, I pushed in the hide-a-bed and resettled the cushions. Flipping on a nature documentary, I made my way to the small kitchen for some Honey Nut O's.

Back on the sofa, I took my first bite. Crunch, crunch, crunch… Odd, it didn't taste quite right. Maybe I didn't seal the bag and it was stale or something. I choked it down anyway and went back to clean up my mess.

Moving through my ritual in the shower, I noticed tenderness on the right side of my throat. Stepping out, I tucked the towel around my torso and peered into the mirror. My eyes were the color of the ocean—not quite like their normal sea green—and my skin was flawless. At least I no longer looked like the walking dead from last night.

Leaning against the small vanity to check my neck, I found two dot-like bruises. Hmm, I must have been bitten by a bug last night.

Swiping on a quick coat of mascara, I perused my closet. My go-to size-4 skinny jeans were loose, and I had to adjust the straps on my favorite C-cup bra. Even my lucky V-necked shirt was baggy. Weird.

Styling my locks, I noticed more of a silver sheen. Maybe I should go to bed with wet hair more often.

Hooking the front door closed with a ballet flat, I locked it and decided a visit to the thrift store was in order. It was only five blocks away.

I snorted to myself: hopefully I wouldn't get mugged again. It was a good thing I had a small stash of savings.

I trotted down the stairs with a bounce in my step, and my thoughts swirled with possibilities. I loved shopping.

As I neared the main drag of Pacific Beach, I noticed the lights seemed brighter and the sounds had more depth. The ocean even smelled sweeter. Maybe that crack to the head had adjusted my sensory input? Only then did I realize there wasn't even a bruise on my scalp from the concrete. Shrugging it off, I continued on my way.

A bell chimed overhead as I pushed open the swinging door.

The bohemian-dressed teen at the register waved hello.

Smiling back, I began searching through the size-2 racks and small tops. My thoughts rolled. Bar… check. Drink… check. The jukebox… check. Another drink… check. Paying… check. Getting lost in my own failures on the fuzzy walk home… check. Then nothing until I was rudely robbed and left on the grass.

With a bundle of clothes draped over each arm, I chose a fitting room and stripped.

A beautiful stranger stared back in the full-length mirror. Where I wasn't toned before, I had triceps. I could even see my ribs. My waist tapered to a tiny hourglass while my hips flared just enough to attract male attention. Even the globes of my rear seemed perkier. If it wasn't uncouth, I could go braless. Grinning at the thought of the girls bouncing in the breeze, I quickly tried on the other selections.

It didn't seem to matter what I put on, everything looked amazing. This would be my best shopping trip yet.

Arms full of fabric, I skipped to the cashier.

She eyed my selections with approval and gave me my total.

Thumbing out a couple bills from my emergency stash, I paid and grabbed my bags.

In the glass reflection on my way out, I could see the cashier staring after me with a strange look of longing on her face. Weird.

Needing a caffeine fix, I popped into Starbucks. As soon as I stepped up to the counter, the room fell silent. The espresso machines hissed, but everyone just stopped and gawked. I looked around for a moment before I figured out that the object of their fascination was… me.

Feeling uncomfortable with my second-hand purchases, I cleared my throat to order.

The barista immediately snapped to attention.

"A venti mocha frappe, please," I mumbled, reaching into my pocket. As I grabbed a ten, the drink appeared in front of me. Was he trying to give me someone else's order? You could have heard a pin drop as I held out the bill.

The employee looked at my outstretched hand like he didn't know what money was. Dumbfounded, he stared for a few beats. "No charge, miss. Thanks for coming in today."

"Um, okay," I stammered, not even wanting the coffee now. Snatching my drink, I turned and headed toward the door.

Every person's eyes followed me with not just longing, but also jealousy, and… lust.

I rushed the five blocks home in record time. What the hell was that all about?

Locking the door, I plugged in my phone. Flopping onto the sofa, I reflected back on the strangest evening ever. I was a dud, just a normal non-magical person. What was with all the looks?

Venti Mocha Frappe and thrift clothes forgotten on the table, I decided to make popcorn and veg out.

Bed pulled out, comfy clothes on, *Orange* on the TV… Perfect. Exhausted, I nodded off in the middle of the third season.

A surge of panic startled me awake.

Reaching over to the table for my phone, I checked the time: 2:00 a.m. I'd been asleep for about five hours. What had awoken me? I heard nothing but the soft sounds of the TV I had fallen asleep listening to, but inside my gut was screaming.

Something was wrong.

Giselle would be sleeping right now. Maybe I should go check on her? As I debated calling her, a soft tapping sounded on the door. Thoroughly freaked out, I grabbed my bat from the corner by the couch and sat on my knees.

It came again. Tap, tap, tap. After a moment, the handle wiggled.

Panicking, I squinted at the deadbolt in the flickering light of the TV. Locked, I sighed in relief.

Tap, tap, tap, thump.

Heart in my throat, I tiptoed to the door while strangling the Louisville Slugger with my sweat-dampened fingers. My home was just a studio/bath above a detached garage with a stair entry on the side. The door opened outward. If shit hit the fan, maybe I could kick it and surprise whoever the hell was sneaking around on the landing.

Muffled voices quickly aborted that plan.

"...I smell it too," said a man's deep timbre.

"Door's locked... too loud," came a muffled reply.

I looked back toward the phone I left on the coffee table, torn between crossing the distance and listening further.

"The scent... near the old lady's house, we... it out?"

In full-on terror, I gripped the bat in one hand and placed my other on the lock. No way was I letting anyone near Giselle.

Another man replied, "No, Blaze said to check it out, not harass old ladies in the... the night."

I slowly let go of the breath I was holding and released the deadbolt. It made a nearly inaudible click as it resettled from my touch.

Silence.

A moment passed.

Knock, knock.

"We can hear you breathing, mouse. Open up. We just want to have a chat."

I debated answering, when the lock began turning on its own. No! Too slowly, I reached out as it fully disengaged and swung open.

Two huge men stood with their faces shadowed against the dim porch light. Heavily corded with muscle, they seemed as big as mountains to my five-foot-nine frame.

Lifting the weapon higher, I readied my stance to strike whoever entered first. I didn't have much, but this was my home. I wouldn't give it up without a fight.

Their shoulders immediately slumped in unison. I waited a few more moments, but they remained as still as statues on my porch.

I shrilled, "Who are you?" Instantly, I cringed at my pitch.

No response.

Stepping closer, I flipped the overhead light on with my elbow.

Unseeing ocean-colored eyes stared back at me from both of their faces. One had dirty-blond hair, while his partner's was dark as night. Both men were dressed completely in black.

I met the blond's gaze and repeated my question. "Who are you?"

"Von," he rumbled.

"And you?"

"Jake."

My eyes ping-ponged while the two guys remained completely motionless.

Confused, I looked to Von. "Why did you come here?"

Factually, he stated, "Blaze said to investigate a strange lingering scent in PB last night. It's coming from you."

"You can s-smell me?" I stuttered. "My, uh, scent drew you here?" I now leaned more toward creeped out, and my panic lowered a notch.

"Yes," he answered. "We caught it near Starbucks and tracked you back here."

"Why?" I squeaked.

He replied in a monotone, "Blaze told us to find you, see what you were."

I took a step back. They remained where they were as if frozen while my mind raced. Strange things had been happening ever since I left that bar. The people's behavior downtown, now two hulking men had tracked me to my home and were answering my questions as if they were hypnotized.

I raised an eyebrow. "I'm human. What are you?"

"Vampires, of the SoCal Clutch."

Obviously Von could carry on a conversation, but Jake stood next to him like a statue. "Jake, who is Blaze?"

He promptly replied, "The leader of our Clutch."

Inspired by their non-threatening manner, I stared hard at Von. "Stand on one foot."

He immediately lifted a black-clad leg. Surprised, I gawked for a moment before addressing Jake, "You too."

What the hell was I supposed to make of this situation? It was almost comical. I knew of Vampires, but I had certainly never met one. Racking my memories, I searched for anything to explain what was happening. It seemed like I was controlling them. Almost… almost like magic.

I was a dud, non-magical, and abandoned because of it. Now it seemed I had some sort of power, just one I'd never heard of. Adrenaline flooded my veins at the revelation.

Peering at Von, I asked, "What are you going to do when you leave here?"

"Tell Blaze… tell him…" his brow wrinkled in confusion "…that we found a human?" The end of his sentence lifted into a question as if asking my opinion.

It seemed I could impart suggestions. Interesting… "How did you unlock my door?"

Jake answered, "We can do simple magic and manipulate items."

That was freaky. Any Vampire could just stroll into my home? My adrenaline rush came to an abrupt stop as fear took over again.

Both Vampires inhaled in unison. Their gazes turned from blank stares into ones of fierce protection and alternating adoration.

Odd. Shelving their reaction, I continued the interrogation. "How do I stop a Vampire?"

Von nodded. "Wards from Mages are usually placed around the exterior of a home. We cannot cross them."

Jake added, "Stakes, beheading, and fire are also very effective ways to stop a Vampire. We cannot go into direct sunlight, and daylight hours weaken us."

Shifting from foot to foot, I slowly digested their information. What the hell was I supposed to do now? I didn't want this, whatever *this* even was.

Narrowing my eyes, I spoke with feigned confidence. "I think you should leave. Never come back, and do not tell anyone about me, especially Blaze."

Their faces mirrored hurt and confusion like I had just kicked their puppies. Strangely enough, the effect almost made me take back my words, but my safety was paramount. Hmm… could I make it an order?

Clearing my throat, I restated, "Jake, Von, leave my home. Never tell anyone about me. Forget me entirely. You were never here. Is that understood?"

"Yes," they replied in unison. Their faces cleared as they turned away and walked silently down my creaky stairs.

If I hadn't seen them leave with my own eyes, I never would have believed they'd gone.

Predatory, my mind supplied as they faded into the night.

With the bat still clutched in my hand, I questioned my own sanity and closed the door.

There was zero chance of sleep now, so I decided to tidy up my bed and head down to the garage to wash my new clothes. Thank the Goddess Giselle's house was just over two hundred feet away and I could come and go as I pleased. As tragic as it was that she had lost her family, I was very grateful to fill the void that they had left behind, and even more grateful that Giselle filled some of mine in return.

A couple hours later, I finished folding my clothes and checked the time: 4:30 a.m. Deciding to watch some more TV, I soon passed out on the couch.

Janelle Peel

Chapter 2

The same sounds awoke me as the day before. Struggling with the crocheted throw and cushions, I began searching for my phone as it abruptly stopped ringing. I continued the fight with the decades-old sofa, when it chimed again. Finally, I located it beneath the couch and pressed the unlock button. 4:30 p.m. How do I keep sleeping away the day? I wonder, thumbing open the text with the G.

'Hey, hon, feeling better? Dinner's at 6.'

I thought for a moment. We'd barely seen each other all week. I typed back, 'Yup, see you then!'

She replied, ':)'

I began what was becoming my evening ritual instead of the usual morning. The only difference was my excitement to try on the clothes I had purchased.

After a quick shower, I wiped the fog from the mirror and froze. My hair was now completely silver, the stuff girls paid hundreds of dollars for at the salon. Ocean-blue eyes stared back at me. My lashes were fuller and my cheekbones seemed more pronounced. I tried not to be vain, but damn, I looked great! Grinning at my new look, I noticed my teeth even seemed whiter, and my lips were a plump pink.

Shrugging it off as a good night's sleep, I finished getting ready and headed over to Giselle's house.

Even from the entryway of her Spanish-style home, it smelled amazing. I let myself in and hollered a greeting. "Smells awesome, Giselle! I was practically drooling outside!"

I rounded the corner as she was coming in from the back deck.

"Steaks?" I looked at her plate. Usually, I steered away from red meat, but this looked delicious. The ribeye's were grilled to perfection.

She replied with a hesitant look on her face, "I know you normally don't go for them, but I got a really good deal for the diner and decided to try them out."

I smiled. "No, they smell great. I'll try one."

Her face shone as she grinned in approval.

Giselle really was beautiful, in that classic Diane Keaton way. Slightly shorter than I, but with curves in all the right places. The regulars at the diner always stared after her when she made her rounds to the tables.

Setting the platter down, she grabbed the salt and pepper. "Potatoes and corn are ready. Could you set the places?"

"Sure." I quickly busied myself with the familiar task. My mind kept wandering to the steaks. Goddess, when was the last time I ate? My O's the day before? I had forgotten everything with all the crazy weirdness going on. No wonder the steaks smelled divine. I was starving.

We finally sat down and served each other as we had numerous times in the past few months.

She watched me with the expectant look of a mother while I took my first bite. It was rare and still bleeding in the center. I popped it into my mouth and instantly moaned.

Her face lit with a million-watt smile. "I hoped you'd like it. That's it, they're going on the menu."

I mumbled my approval, too engrossed in shoveling in my meal as fast as possible. It felt like I hadn't eaten in a month! Using my potatoes to soak up every drop of juice left on the plate, I took my last bite and leaned back with a contented sigh.

"Whoa! Have a drink, dear," she chided. "You'll choke."

"That was absolutely amazing. Thank you so much. I didn't realize how hungry I was. Food has tasted off lately," I grimaced, thinking about my cereal and forgotten popcorn from the day before.

"Well, you look like you've lost a few pounds. You're not dieting, are you? You know you're gorgeous. All these fads with 'thin' these days." She shook her head in disapproval.

I smiled. "No, no dieting. I feel great, better than great actually."

Her frown turned back into a grin. "You do look amazing. Did you change your hair? I've never seen it so silver."

"Honestly, no. I'm not quite sure what's going on with it, but I love it. I was thinking about cutting it last week, but I'm definitely going to keep it now," I said, running my fingers through the shoulder-length tresses.

"I agree." She beamed. "It's rather lovely on you."

My cheeks heated. "Thanks."

We continued to make small talk while we cleared the table and did the dishes.

Her brows rose as I was getting ready to head out. "Do you have plans tonight?"

"I'm not sure. I think maybe I'll go for a walk on the beach before it gets too late."

She gave me the eye. "Well, you be careful."

Kissing her cheek, I answered, "I will, I will, promise." She was such a mother hen.

We made our usual date for next Wednesday.

It was chilly again as I burrowed deeper into my jacket. The Moon shone off the water and highlighted the breaking waves. The ocean smelled so crisp.

Sinking my bare toes into the cold sand, I thought over everything that had happened. I needed answers. Grabbing my sandals, I decided to visit my only friend and hit her froyo cafe to do some research.

The door chimed overhead as it announced my arrival. Wiping my salty, sandy sandals on the rug, I glanced around. It was closer to nine, closing time, and the place was deserted. Frozen treats on a chilly night just weren't as enticing as the coffee shop around the corner.

Viv popped her head out from behind the counter and yelled over the loud music, "Hey, stranger!"

She stood at five foot nothing with her two-inch pink hair spiked out every direction possible. Her tiny figure was lost in the large yellow apron looped twice around her frame. Green eyes sparkling, a devious grin slid over her lips as she scanned me from head to toe. Chucks slapping against the tiled floor, she made her way over and gave me a bone-crushing hug.

For a tiny thing, she sure was strong.

I grinned down at her. "Hey, what happened to the Rainbow Dash look?" My chin bumped against a pink spike as I released her.

"Everyone has blue, purple, and pink these days," she answered with a disgusted look on her face. Viv always liked to stand out in a crowd. Her hot-magenta lips shifted into a mock pout. "What brings you in? I hardly ever see you anymore unless I come to the diner."

"I know, sorry." I cringed. "I've just been dealing with some family things. Me and all my baggage, right?" My attempt at a smile fell flat. Viv was an orphan; she understood being on your own. Despite losing her parents at a young age, she came back stronger than ever from it. She only knew my parents were gone, not that I was practically a leper among my people.

"Well, I have the perfect fix for that." She smiled, grabbing a paper bowl from the counter. Expertly working the chrome levers on the machine, she poured my usual froyo. "Chocolate fixes everything."

She was infectious.

"Of course it does."

"You look good, been working out? I see you're finally wearing some nice stuff." She wagged her brows at me. "New boyfriend?"

"Yeah, no." I paused. "Just been trying some new things."

She winked. "Nice. Well, you eat that. I have a few things to do before I can lock up."

Closing consisted of stacking chairs and texting her boyfriend to tell him their plans for the night. I envied her normal life and cheery persona.

"Actually, um, could I borrow your laptop?" My brows lifted hopefully. "I have some things I want to research."

"Sure. I'm out of here in thirty minutes though. Is that okay?"

"Perfect, thanks." I sighed in relief and made my way to her office.

Shutting the door, I sat in her chair. The Apple computer was already on, so I just popped into the internet search engine and came to an abrupt stop. What the heck was I even supposed to look up? A Clutch? Vampires? Mind control?

I typed away, using different searches and keywords before I promptly began to panic. There was nothing. What was I thinking? Sure, there were plenty of fanatic sites. Even blood-drinking ones; but nothing beyond books and folklore. Everything on mind control was layered in psychic crap and the occult. This was a colossal waste of time and my thirty minutes were up. Damn. Clearing the browser history, I got up just as Viv was coming in.

She nodded to the computer. "Find what you needed?"

"Not really. Just looking up some family stuff."

She frowned in sympathy and looped an arm around my waist. "It gets easier, you know?"

I smiled. "I hope so."

"Hey, you didn't eat your ice cream. Does it taste okay?" She frowned, spooning at the melted brown mess inside the bowl.

"It's fine. I just had a huge dinner with Giselle and don't have anywhere to put it." I reached out and pinched her jutting hip bone, with a wink.

She giggled. "Okay. Just toss it. Jason will be here in a few. We're heading out for a couple drinks. Want to come?"

Shrugging, I bit my lip. "Thanks, but I have an early shift tomorrow. No rest for the weary." I hated lying to her. I was scheduled for the lunch shift, not breakfast. If she was going out, I doubted she'd pop in before that. "Do you need any help locking up?"

"No, I got it. You'd better get home and get some sleep. Those early hours suck." She crossed her eyes at the thought of waking before six o'clock.

"All right, take care. Don't do anything I wouldn't do." I thrust my hips in a mock dance move.

We both cracked up. My moves were nonexistent. I danced like a newborn colt frolicking in a field on shaky legs.

Janelle Peel

As the door closed behind me, and Viv clicked the lock on the other side, a feeling of unease slithered down my spine. I looked around, but only saw a few people with their eyes glued to their phones or engrossed in conversation. The street lights were bright, but I couldn't shake the feeling of being watched. I debated calling a Lyft home, but decided against it. With my tips stolen, I didn't want to dip any further into my meager savings.

As I made my way into the dimmer suburbs, the feeling neither grew stronger nor subsided.

Six more blocks to go.

Rounding the next corner, I spotted a man on the other side of the street walking in the same direction. It was too dark to make out anything other than his blond hair, but I kept an eye on him in my peripheral vision until he turned at the next street. Relieved, I sighed. I did not need another encounter with a stranger. Lengthening my stride, I picked up my pace to get home.

Approaching my studio, I noticed my porch light wasn't on. It must have burnt out, I thought, climbing the steps. Slipping the key into the lock, I turned the handle, when I was overwhelmed with a dose of adrenaline. Fight or flight.

Someone was in my house.

I jerked the door open in a panic, but no one was there. Flipping the deadbolt, I quickly checked the bathroom and tiny shower.

Nothing.

Heart rate calming, I walked back to the kitchen area. Opening the mini fridge, I felt a draft against the nape of my neck. Slowly, I turned.

A brick of a man stood in my open entryway.

I gasped. Lowering my gaze, I eyed my bat near the door from my last encounter.

His lips tilted into a smirk as if daring me to go for it.

He had a strong jawline and high cheekbones. Not pretty, but handsome in a bad-boy kind of way. The jacket he wore was open to a dark blue T-shirt. Faded jeans finished the look paired with black combat boots.

He stared.

I stared. It was like a Wild West standoff.

After a moment, I injected feigned confidence into my voice. "Who the hell are you, and what are you doing in my house?"

His lips curled into a full devilish smile that dimpled his cheeks. Deep, rich laughter rolled out, immediately pissing me off.

Squaring my shoulders, I stalked toward him with a glare. His teeth snapped closed when I was a foot from him… and my weapon.

Catching the movement of my eyes, he growled, "I wouldn't."

Crossing my arms as a barrier, I tried to ignore the fluttering of my stomach. "Answer me!"

Inside, a silent demand screamed, *Let go*.

So, I did. Brilliant blue light lit my hands, dancing across my knuckles as I spread each finger. The glow played across the stranger's face as he stared, completely transfixed by whatever the hell I was doing.

This close, I could smell him. Clean and crisp like the ocean, and very similar to my home back in Seattle. Inhaling again, I licked my lips and relaxed into the memory.

He flared his nostrils as his gaze tracked the motion. Shock and recognition flashed across his face. "You."

Confusion coursed through me. I didn't know this mountain of a man that smelled like home. Returning his assessment, I noted how his leather jacket clung to him like a second skin. Focus!

Tossing my hair over one shoulder, I asked, "Do I know you?"

Stepping back, he overcame his previous emotional slip with the movement. "I'm Blaze, Master of the SoCal Clutch." One perfect brow rose. "And you are?"

I shook out my hands in hopes of extinguishing the flames. As they winked out, I bit out, "Sora," to cover my surprise.

"Sora," he whispered.

The longing in his voice made my heart beat faster.

Clearing his throat, he murmured, "Can I come in?"

Appalled at my body's reaction, I snarked, "It's a little late for pleasantries now, isn't it? You already manipulated my door and let yourself in. Now you're asking permission?"

"Yes," he rumbled back, following with a lower, "please."

I debated for a moment. I have magic! Magic… that I didn't know how to use…. Oh well, fake it 'til you make it.

"Fine," I answered, tipping my head to the couch.

He silently strode across the room and settled himself on the sofa like he was afraid to break it. The hide-a-bed groaned a loud complaint, but held. His bulk took up so much space, I remained standing.

I crossed my arms again. "What do you want?"

He let out a long sigh. "I came to investigate a scent I noticed early last night. I sent two of my best Trackers to hunt down whatever it was, only to have them fail to report back. When I tracked them down, they had no clue of the order I issued. Like their memory was wiped." He leaned forward, and the couch whined its disdain at the abuse. "Any idea why that is?"

My thoughts scrambled as my pulse skyrocketed.

His pupils dilated. Tracing the curve of my jaw, they came to rest on my fluttering jugular.

My quick intake of breath caused him to look away. Chagrined, he muttered, "Sorry."

Vampire, right. Gulping past the lump in my throat, I debated on the best answer that wouldn't betray my weird ability. An ability that didn't seem to work on him.

Ignorance was bliss. I quipped, "What are you talking about?"

His eyes turned cold as his gaze swung back to mine. "You really want to play that game?" Thick muscles flexed beneath his coat, straining the material in a mesmerizing display of masculinity. The threat was clear in every line of his hard body.

My eyes widened as fear shot through me.

Drawing in a short burst of air, he seemed to relax. I diverted, "Why do you breathe?"

His brow furrowed as if he was thrown by the abrupt change in topic. "To gather scents, speak, and blend in."

Okay… I wonder what he smells? My own senses had increased ever since I cracked my head after the bar… Wait! Curley's! The blond man with the strong jaw. It was him! "Have I seen you before?"

Rolling his shoulders into a shrug, he contemplated my question. "I believe we were at the same establishment the other night."

I threw my arms up in exasperation. "Establishment! Yeah, establishment. Let's go with that."

His sarcasm matched mine. "You were also there, alone, as I recall. Painting it black, right?"

Venomously, I spat, "It's a classic."

Rising, he towered over me. "You're stalling. Tell me what I want to know."

Shit, he must be six foot three or more. Never had I felt so crowded by a man that smelled so damned good, in all my life.

Noting my reaction, he turned toward the window and addressed my reflection. "Please, just tell me what I want to know."

His sincerity undid me. "Two guys, Von and Jake, broke into my home. I don't know what they wanted. I had my bat. They left. I don't know what happened to them after. End of story." I mentally crossed my fingers for him to believe my edited version of events.

His sigh fogged the glass.

Holding my breath, I waited.

"Fine," he growled. As he prowled to the door, his shitkickers made hollow noises of displeasure on my thin carpet. Hand on the handle, he glanced back condescendingly. "Know this, Mage: there are others that reside in SoCal that will have caught your unique scent and will come to investigate. Others not so patient as I." In a move too quick to follow, he tossed a card onto my coffee table. "Call if you require assistance. Good night, Sora."

I blinked. My door was closed and locked as if he'd never been there at all.

Blaze

Never had he been so frustrated by a female, nor had he been so turned on by scent alone either. Her mint shampoo played nicely to the delicate tones of surf and lavender. That alone was odd; ocean scents usually identified Vampires. Perhaps it was residual from his bite two nights before, or even the Trackers he sent. She certainly wasn't a Vampire…

Mentally, he replayed the toss of her hair… like liquid silver. His hand trembled with the urge to run his fingers through it.

"Sora," he whispered into the wind.

The Moon had fully risen by the time he settled in to watch her home from a broken streetlight.

Sora

What the hell was that? Why couldn't I control him like the other two? Maybe it was his leadership to their Clutch. He radiated power like most women overused perfume. Picking up the card, I read it while peeking out the window to the street.

Deeply engraved in black on thick white paper, it read,

BLAZE

619.440.1667

My thumb rolled over the indentations. Pfft, not even a last name? Weird.

Checking the view once more, I moved to the poor hide-a-bed and racked my brain for any memory on warding.

Nothing came to mind. That was the trick with magic: you couldn't learn to use it unless you had it. Why did this have to happen now? Recalling the blue flames, I surmised it had to have been instinctive due to my heightened emotions.

Clasping my hands, I closed my lids and searched for the pull I felt earlier. There, near my center, was an azure light. Gently, oh so gently, I coaxed it out and opened my eyes.

Holy shit! Surprised, I inspected the bright flames. Would they burn everything?

Hesitantly, I touched my hair. Nothing. My palm lowered to the table with the same results.

Emboldened, I walked to the door and concentrated on never letting anyone in without permission. Gliding my fingers over the frame and base, I came to rest on the knob itself. Over and over I repeated that no one shall enter without permission. On the third repeat, I felt a shift in my chest. The trim and handle lit with first blue, then white light. It flared once before extinguishing without a mark.

Magic! I did a mini dance to mark the occasion. Feeling slightly dizzy, I stumbled over to the couch, pulled a blanket over myself, and fell asleep.

Janelle Peel

Chapter 3

Sora

Ding… ding… Ding… ding…
    I lifted my sleep-crusted lids.
    DING…
What? Snatching my cell from the table, I quickly silenced the shrill tone.

Ugh, I groaned into the pillow. My shift at the diner.

Rolling to stand, I folded my blanket. Padding to the bathroom, the events of the previous night jolted me back to reality.

Oh shit!

Hands covering my face, I peered through my fingers and willed it all to be a dream. The puffy blue-green eyes in the mirror and crazy bedhead did nothing to reassure me.

Flipping on the shower, I pushed the problems to the back of my mind. I could figure it out later; I needed this job and my home.

I clocked in at 10:59 without paying attention to anyone and nodded my good mornings to the other wait staff. Tying on my backup apron, I headed out to my six-booth section.

Arriving at the first table, I finally looked up.

Two large men stared at me. Each flared their nostrils as they inhaled in unison.

Noticing for the first time the silence of the room, I glanced around. Not a fork scraped nor a menu crinkled. Everyone was staring, again. Heat rushed to my face as my shoulders rounded. Staring hard at my order tablet, with my pen poised, I cleared my throat. "What can I get you?"

The tanned guy on the left shifted on the brown vinyl. "Black coffee."

Closing his menu, the other man muttered, "Same, with the Steak Skillet. Rare, white toast."

Nodding, I scribbled the order down, plucked their menus from the table, and beat a hasty retreat to the kitchen.

The elderly cook looked up with a smile as I handed him the ticket. "Rough start?" His head tipped to the pass-through window. "Those boys aren't giving you trouble, are they?"

Thankful for the normalcy, I met his eyes with a grin. "No, just the usual."

Near instantly, his eyes glazed over. Shaking himself, he mumbled, "I'll get this together. You better get back out there."

"Um, thanks," I uttered, pushing through the swinging door to the server station. I could do this. So, people were staring. Who cared? I had to get over these strange encounters. Time to kick ass and get paid.

Pep talk done, I poured two cups of Columbian Black. People continued to gawk as I retraced my footsteps to the booth.

Setting the coffees down, Skillet Guy addressed me with his brows lowered in thought. "You new here?"

"Nope, I've been here for about four months. This your first trip in?"

"No, Mel and I have been coming here for years. We've just never noticed your sc…" he corrected himself quickly "…smiling face before."

Thoughts whirling, I tilted my chin toward "Mel." "You decide on any food yet?"

Blowing over his raised cup, he shrugged. "Coffee's good, thanks."

"All right then, I'll be back with your food in a bit. If you need more coffee just set your mug"—I patted the table—"on the end here."

Turning away, I moved on. The stares and stammers were easier to handle after that. Lifting my lips, I waited as patiently as I could.

A ding sounded as Skillet Guy's food appeared in the window. I shuffled ketchup and A1 into one hand, grabbed a rack of jelly with my pinky, and double plated the skillet and toast with my other.

He was talking animatedly with his hands. Mel stared back with a glare on his face. At my approach, they fell silent.

Janelle Peel

Placing everything on the plastic surface, I injected fake cheer into my voice. "Here you go. Will there be anything else?"

They shook their heads.

"All right, here's your check. Flag me down if you change your minds."

First the scent thing, then the weird silence. Shelving the thoughts, I finished my shift on autopilot.

As I was getting ready to leave, the hostess snagged my shoulder with adoration lighting her hazel eyes.

"Hey, the first guys you served left your tip up front when they paid. There's a couple others as well, but theirs stood out." She handed over a white envelope with my name on it.

Slipping my fingers inside, I pulled out a fifty and a few other bills. Scrawled on the fifty were the words, "Call me, Mel 6197741282." I gasped. "Did they say anything?"

"Nope, the other guy paid the tab, and his friend left that for you." She wagged her brows. "They were pretty cute."

"Um, thanks. I guess they were." I waved over my shoulder. "See you tomorrow."

Shoving the envelope and cash into the pocket of my apron, I rushed home.

It was early evening by the time I closed the door to my studio. Placing my hand on the handle, I tried to feel any energy from the ward. A slight hum met my fingertips. Cool, it must mean it's still active.

Walking to the couch, I untied my apron and emptied its contents onto the coffee table. Sitting down, I gawked. That was a lot of cash. Grabbing the remote, I turned on the local news and started counting.

Two hundred and fifty-six dollars for a six-hour shift. Whoa. Never had I received so many tips in one day.

Thumbing out most of the stack, I made my way to the mini fridge. Opening the freezer, I pulled out my zip lock of savings. Pinching my pennies was doing me well, but a few more shifts like this and I could afford a vacation. *If* I had somewhere to go.

Replacing the bag, I glanced down at the frozen meals. I still wasn't hungry, and nothing looked remotely appetizing. Hip checking the door closed, I padded back to the couch.

Multiple strange men, all affected by my scent, and two phone numbers. Mel couldn't have been a Vampire; it was daylight.

What the hell was going on?

I scribbled his phone number on the back of Blaze's card.

Mind spinning with confusion, I decided to take a hot shower.

As I stepped out of the foggy bathroom, a knock sounded on the front door.

"Who is it?"

Another knock came.

"Who is it?" I repeated, pitching my voice louder.

No response.

Hanging my towel on the hook, I slipped into my grey terry-cloth robe. Padding to the entry, I shouted, "WHO IS IT?"

The knob shook in tandem with a man's muffled curse.

Simultaneously, I felt a tiny pinch in my chest.

Grabbing my bat, I flicked the lock and pushed it open.

Mel from the diner stood on my porch holding his hand to his wide chest.

Glancing past him, I asked, "What the hell are you doing here? At my house?"

His chocolate eyes widened at my robe but dismissed the bat entirely. I shifted its position, but he didn't notice it.

Clearing his throat, he shook out his fingers. "I've come to issue a request on behalf of the SoCal Pack."

Wait, what? Dumbfounded, I stared at him.

He blinked. "I am the Alpha of the SoCal Pack."

My face screwed up as I tried to grasp memories long forgotten. A Pack… like Shifters?

I took him in from head to toe. His brown hair curled at the tops of his ears. Wearing an untucked grey polo, khaki board shorts, and… Wait. Were those green flip-flops? My mind stuttered to a stop. Flip-flops…on a Shifter. A manic giggle slipped past my lips.

He glanced at his feet. "What?" Blushing furiously, he grouched, "They're easy to slip off for a shift."

This was just too insane! I laughed, long and loud. His face hardened at the ridicule.

Tears streamed down my cheeks, and a giggle snorted through my nose.

Tentatively, he smiled.

Slapping my palm over my mouth, I grinned. "I'm sorry, it's just been a long week."

He fidgeted. "I hoped you would call."

My hackles rose. Cocking a hip, I snarked, "You put your number on a tip. That does *not* mean I have to call you. Obviously you sniffed me out though. What do you want?"

He gestured inside. "Can we talk?"

Incredulous, I answered, "Um, no? I'm in a robe. It's nighttime. What sane woman invites a strange man into her home after he's stalked her?"

Flexing his fingers, he stared down at his reddened palm.

I hesitated. "What happened to your hand?"

Ears reddening, he muttered, "Your, um, door burned me when I tried to open it."

"So not only did you stalk me, you tried to enter my home?" I glared. "You need to leave."

"No, please, just listen. Hear me out."

He reached out to the door frame. A sharp pain lanced my chest as he made contact. The entire frame glowed blue, then white. Fire raced across the open space as it made a solid flame.

BOOM!

I fell back on my rear, completely unprepared for the concussion. Blinking hard to clear the spots from my vision, I shakily stood and peered outside. The landing was empty, save for one lone green sandal. Leaning further out, I looked around.

There, sprawled on the grass, awkwardly trying to move its forelegs, was the biggest brown Wolf I had ever seen. As he noticed my gaze, his upper lip rose to reveal one very large, finger-sized fang. He was not happy.

Taking a sharp breath at his reaction, I smelled burnt hair. His left leg was bald and smoking.

He rumbled a vicious growl before loping off into the darkness.

Shuddering at the mess my life had become, I gently closed the door. I ran my fingers over the panel, and the ward hummed as I thanked the Goddess the frame wasn't damaged.

It was a damned good thing Giselle was at work tonight. That was the last thing I needed.

Tucking my legs beneath my sore rear on the couch, I debated picking up the phone. Blaze said to call if I required assistance. He knew others would catch my scent.

Shit.

Blaze

He grinned as he watched the charred Wolf retreat to lick his wounds.

Sora seemed to be handling herself well enough.

He wasn't sure why he returned after dusk. Something about her called to him. If he was honest with himself, it wasn't just her scent. Ocean-colored eyes in a perfectly sculpted face. High cheekbones paired with full pink pouty lips. He yearned to touch her silver hair. Christ, she even managed to make a bathrobe look seductive as it molded to her soft curves.

Her anger at the Wolf turned him on; the crisp bite of sea water was more pronounced with her outrage. Licking his lips, he replayed the memory of her taste. She'd only smelled mildly of the ocean then, he mused. It's what caught his attention at the bar.

Settling back on the balls of his feet, he waited for her call.

Sora

After making my favorite brand of coffee and pouring it into a chipped mug, I debated whether or not to call Blaze. I took a sip, and my stomach soured. Instantly, I spit it back into the cup. Damn it. Dumping the ruined drink in the sink, I rinsed the mug and set it back on the rack.

Pulling out my sleep shorts and tank from my tiny linen closet, I quickly dressed. Padding to the bathroom, I grabbed a comb from the vanity and headed to my window seat. Untangling the messy strands, I watched my reflection in the glass.

With a sigh, I reached for my phone and hovered my thumb over the keys.

Screw it.

Punching in his number, I half hoped to get voicemail after the third ring.

"Yes?" a deep voice rumbled, making my stomach flip.

"Hey, Blaze? Um uh, hi. It's Sora." I cringed.

His tone was all business. "What is it?"

"Well, you said I could call, that others would come…" My voice lowered to a whisper. "That I might require assistance?"

The pause on the other end was so long, I checked the phone's display to make sure it hadn't lost signal.

Finally, after what seemed an eternity, he replied, "What do you need?"

Goddess, he was going to make me ask for help. Screw that! I snarked, "Well, you tell me. I didn't ask for any of this crap."

He chuckled.

Butterflies danced in my belly at the rich sound. Holding my breath, I waited for him to say something, anything.

Knock, knock.

I jumped and nearly fell off my chair. Who the hell was here now? It was like Grand Central Station around here.

"Well," his voice came through the door a second before the speaker pressed against my ear, "are you going to let me in?"

Shit, he was here? Now? Hitting End, I walked to the door. Taking a moment to compose myself, I flipped the lock and pushed it open.

My eyes widened as I took in his tall, muscular form. Goddess, he looked good. His eyes seemed almost black in the low light, further enhanced by the thick fan of lashes against his cheeks. My heart beat faster while I slowly looked my fill from his boots to his chin.

Clearing his throat, the corner of one lip lifted as if my perusal amused him.

Stepping aside, I tucked my chin to hide my blush. "Please, come in."

As he prowled through the doorway, his denim jeans flexed with every step. Without the leather jacket, his black T-shirt looked painted on. It highlighted the perfect *v* of his hips.

Inhaling through my nose, I parsed his scent while closing the door. He smelled delicious. *Home*, my body screamed.

He turned toward me. "Well?"

My mouth ran dry. Swallowing, I quipped, "That was fast. Are you still stalking me?"

Returning my glib, he stepped within inches of my chest. "If I am?"

My body betrayed me as I leaned toward him. What? No, focus!

Rocking back on my heels, I shook my head. "Then you know why I called. What the hell is going on?"

He silently strode toward the couch and sat. A smile lit his face when it once again squealed its dissent. "I came to check up on you. I saw the Wolf; nice work there." His eyes flashed to cobalt as if he truly enjoyed the show.

My heart warmed at the praise, and I snickered, "It was pretty funny." Instantly, I sobered. I needed answers, not admiration from a Vampire I barely knew. "Please, just tell me what is going on."

Poker face in place, he replied, "Tit for tat, if you want information."

I walked to the window and sat. I had to keep my distance from him. Never had a male affected me so drastically before, nor had I met one that changed moods so quickly.

Hesitantly, I asked, "What do you want to know?"

He lifted a brow. "Where are you from?"

Sliding a pony tie off my wrist, I tipped my head back and gathered my damp tresses to begin a loose braid over one shoulder. Watching my fingers work the strands, I muttered, "Seattle. I kind of migrated down the coast and ended up here." Raising my eyes to his, I noticed he was staring at my neck. He quickly averted his gaze, but not before I saw the need reflected in his dark depths.

Tying off the end, I bounced my leg and pondered my own question. "Why are you stalking me? I mean, um, what is so interesting about my scent? First your Trackers, then you, and now a Shifter."

He nodded in anticipation. "Your scent is unique, as I said before. You smell of the ocean, with hints of mint and lavender. It's intoxicating." He sighed. "The kicker is, only Vampires smell like the sea. That brings us to my next question. What are you?"

His eyes were so earnest, I found I did want to tell someone of my past. Taking a deep breath, I began, "I was born to some of the most powerful Mages in the Seattle Stronghold. It was assumed I would be incredibly powerful. Most come into their power at puberty. I didn't." Raising a shoulder, I tried to push down the hurricane of negative emotions. "My parents tried everything. Tutors, enhanced spell books, hypnotism. Our Seer couldn't see me, or my future. I was just a blank space, void of magic, worthless. On my twenty-first birthday, my parents were called before the Council. I'm not sure what was said, but I was kicked out of my home because I had no magic. My mother and father were so embarrassed, they didn't even say goodbye. I was left like trash on the curb, alone, with nothing but the clothes on my back in Downtown Seattle." I met his azure gaze as he leaned forward with interest. At least it wasn't a look of sympathy, thank the Goddess. "You see, I didn't have magic until after that night at the bar."

He frowned.

My brow furrowed. "I'm not really sure what I am. Do you know?"

His granite mask slid back into place as he shifted back to his original position. "I have some theories, but I'm not prepared to share them yet. I need to do some research first. Do you have any other questions, so we can continue?"

"Yes. What do you think Mel, the Wolf Shifter, wanted?"

His entire body flexed as his torso rotated toward me. The churning ocean on a moonless night darkened his irises in disapproval. "Mel was the Wolf? The one charred by your ward?"

I stammered at the abrupt change. "Ye-yes. He came to the d-diner where I work today. He had some other guy with him. He wrote his number on a fifty-dollar bill and left it with the cashier." My shoulders rounded as the menace radiating from him increased. "He stalked me home and said he wanted to issue a request. He wanted to come in to talk, but I refused. He put his hand on the doorframe, and boom" —I threw out my arms— "the ward activated. It blasted him off my landing and across the yard."

Standing, he barked, "We need to leave."

Struck dumb by the entire exchange, I stared.

His boots clomped loudly in agitation as he stepped toward me.

Cringing away in fear, I turned to the side while closing my eyes for the blow that was sure to come.

Instead, he placed his fingertips under my chin and gently tipped my face up. Once I met his gaze, he rumbled, "I will never hurt you."

His face scrunched in anger and disgust as if the mere thought offended him.

"We have to leave. That Wolf is the Alpha of the SoCal Pack. This slight, accidental as it was, will not be forgiven. He will come back with reinforcements and force you to do whatever he requires. We must go. I cannot deal with thirty Wolves on my own." He paused before adding, "Or their Mage."

Heart racing, I asked, "A Mage? Go where?"

Releasing his grip, he growled, "My Clutch."

My posture changed to defend what was mine as I stood. "What about my home? Giselle? I can't just leave!"

"Your presence does nothing but endanger the old woman. Ward everything, but we have to leave. NOW!" His voice boomed in the tiny space, leaving no room for argument.

I ran to the linen closet and pulled out a rolled-up duffel bag. Throwing in half of my clothes and my makeup pouch from the bathroom, I pivoted and snagged my jacket off the back of the couch. Shoving my arms through the sleeves, I stomped to my mini fridge and grabbed my savings. No way was I leaving without that. Dashing past the couch, I tugged my charger from the wall and pocketed my phone.

Blaze tapped his impatience on the window frame while staring intently into the night.

"Ready," I bit out, glaring at his back. It had only taken me a moment to pack. My chest ached at the thought of leaving the only place I felt any peace since I was kicked out of my home. I was livid.

"Good. Outside, go. You need to ward the perimeter." Turning on his heel, he opened the door and pushed me through. His magic snicked the lock after us as he tugged me down the stairs.

I scoffed, "How the hell do I do that?"

"Figure out how you did it the first time," he hazarded a guess, "but bigger."

What the fuck? Damn it! Cursing the Vampire at my side, I squatted to the ground. Closing my eyes, I imagined a large rectangular shape big enough to cover the garage and Giselle's home, but small enough to leave the sidewalk untouched. Holding the image firmly in my mind, I placed my hands in the dirt. No one will enter without her or my permission. I held her face prominently in my mind, glossing over her silver-streaked hair and warm smile before I reached for my center. My hands immediately lit with blue flame. Opening my lids, I struggled to concentrate on the ward and her. Slowly, the flame lit the grass. Gently, it flickered in the breeze. With one last mental repeat of my will, it shot off into the night like it was following a trail of gasoline. It hit the first corner of the house while I rose to my feet. A heartbeat later, the flames came rushing toward me from behind the garage. As they met the start, the circuit completed and flashed a foot-high, sapphire flame. A second later, it turned a brilliant white before winking out without a trace.

My chest ached with the expenditure of power. I squatted back down and reached back into the damp soil. Pride ran through my thoughts as the hum of magic coursed through the soil and tickled my palm.

Blaze pulled me to standing.

Completely exhausted, I swayed. A Wolf yipped on the wind as I passed out against him.

Chapter 4

Sora

A voice broke through the nightmare as large snapping teeth slowly gave way to softly whispered words.

Swimming to consciousness, I evaluated my body. Goddess, my head hurt. My stomach was trying to eat its way through my spleen. When was the last time I ate?

Lying on possibly the most comfortable bed in the world, I inhaled. It smelled like home.

Home... what?

Snapping my lids open, I immediately located Blaze sitting near the foot of the bed on a black leather wingback. The ankle of one scuffed combat boot draped over his knee as he dwarfed the chair beneath him.

Nodding toward me, he spoke louder into the phone. "No, I don't care... Send one of the

Menagerie.... I know... no, it must be at least an inch thick... A few pounds, yes... Right, the thickest cuts... Good." His phone made an audible clicking tone as he ended the call.

Eyeing him from my prone position, I croaked, "Water."

He tipped his head toward the side table, and his blond hair slid over one eye with the movement.

Asshole. Sitting up proved difficult. My muscles twanged at the abuse. It felt like I had run a marathon. I gave him the stink eye as my seeking fingers finally curled around the glass. Bringing it to my parched mouth, I slowly sipped.

Clearing my sore throat, I snarked, "What happened?"

"You passed out. Too much magic for your newly awakened powers would be my guess. I had to carry you here."

Still dressed in my tank and shorts, I fingered the soft grey duvet tucked in around me. Looking around the room, I noted I was on a king-sized bed. The walls were a light grey, and nothing like the cheery canary of my home. Home. My gaze drifted to the vacant fireplace and nickel wall sconces. "Where is here, exactly?"

Cobalt eyes twinkling, he smirked. "My room."

"Your room," I murmured. Breathing through my mouth to shut out the familiarity around me, I pretended nonchalance. "How long was I out?"

"Just the night. It's seven in the morning." He glanced at the blacked-out window with a lost expression. "I always know where the sun is."

Shelving his reaction, I shuddered in remembrance of my dreams. "Did the Shifters come?"

He tipped his head back to rest on the chair. "Yes. It was close. Too close."

We sat in silence while I tried to make sense of the next step.

A knock at the door startled me from my plans.

"Enter," Blaze commanded.

The handle turned.

Before I knew what was happening, I was out of bed and pulling the door open. The aroma of fresh grilled steak was too strong to deny. I snatched the plate from the alarmed man like a rabid animal and licked my lips. His strange look slowed my movements. "So sorry," I muttered as a blush lit my cheeks, "I don't know what came over me." That was embarrassing. I swallowed hard against the saliva pooling in my mouth.

He smiled tentatively. "No problem, miss." Bypassing me, he moved to the side table. "You must be famished." Setting the tray down, he turned to the wingback. "Will there be anything else, Master Blaze?"

Master, huh? Rolling my eyes, I stalked to the bed and began busying myself with arranging the setting over my legs.

Blaze's amusement colored his reply. "No, thank you, Julian. That will be all."

The door had barely closed before I was stuffing barely cut-up bites of rare heaven into my mouth as fast as possible. The bed dipped, and I almost growled, *MINE*. Mine? The thought snapped me out of my haze. Where the hell did that come from?

I looked down at the remains of my steak.

Of what must have originally been two pounds of meat, only the fatty edge remained. I fought back the urge to lick the blood off the plate. Sighing softly in contentment, I sat back while Blaze removed the tray.

Pinching the napkin in one large hand, he strode toward the door and placed the setting outside. I caught a glimpse of silver-lined wallpaper in the hall as it closed. Silently, he walked back to my side and reached toward my face.

I instantly pulled away.

His eyes flashed black before he set the cloth on the table. Turning away, he moved back to his post on the chair. "You have blood on your cheek."

Cheeks heating, I grabbed the napkin and mopped my face. The blush traveled to the tips of my ears as I looked at the evidence of my savagery. Trying not to die of embarrassment, I met his eyes through my lowered lashes. "Have you had a chance to do any research?"

He nodded. Thankfully, he didn't draw any further attention to my animalistic behavior. His mask slid into place. "Yes, although we have a few things to discuss before I get to that."

I found myself missing the smirk. If he was going to do all business, I could too. Stifling the urge to stick my tongue out, I requested calmly, "Well, I have to work today. Can we address that issue first?"

He shook his head. "You can't go back to work. You need to come up with an excuse to take a leave of absence."

"What!" I exclaimed, losing my poker face. "I can't do that! What about my home? Money? Giselle?"

"Unless you want to essentially be a slave for Mel, you will. As I told you last night, your presence will only endanger anyone you knew before." His tone was neither mocking or jovial. It was simply a fact.

My thoughts bounced around inside my skull. How could I leave the life I had just barely built? I loved Giselle like a mother. What could I say to make her understand? I didn't want to be anyone's slave. Slapping my curled fists onto the bed, I shouted, "I can't just leave everything!"

He raised a perfectly sculpted eyebrow at my outburst and patiently waited for me to come to the only logical conclusion.

Why did he have to be so reasonable? I wanted a fight, and he just sat there, waiting. Damn it all! Taking a few deep breaths, my shoulders slumped in defeat against the plush pillows. I guess I could have a family emergency, some lost relative or whatever. Giselle never pried about my life before; she assumed my parents were dead.

I sighed. "How long?"

He braced his elbows on his knees. "I don't know. A few weeks at least."

"Weeks," I whispered, closing my eyes against the ache inside of my chest. Resigned, I uttered, "I need a phone."

A thump drew my attention to the bed. He'd tossed my Nokia near my hip.

Irritated by his uncaring attitude, I snapped, "Um, some privacy?"

Slowly, he stood. His large build made the big room seem smaller. I tried not to cower as I remembered that he was an apex predator. Staring hard at the bed, I grasped my cell as he departed.

With shaking fingers, I found her number. Tears blurred my vision as I connected the call.

"Hey, hon! Good morning," she cheered. "I was just getting ready to text you. I know you work the lunch rush today, but I thought maybe we could get together for dinner tonight? I have someone I'd like you to meet."

My thoughts screeched to a halt. Who could she have met? If anyone took advantage of her from the fucked-up parts of my life… My left hand flared with blue flame as my magic instantly responded to my anger.

Shaking out the flames, I tried to inject enthusiasm into my voice. "You met someone?"

"Yes! His name is Gary. He's a longtime friend of mine. I finally decided I've grieved enough and want to try for some happiness with the years I have left."

Oh, thank the All Mother. A longtime friend. She sounded so happy, I hated myself for ruining it. "That's amazing; you totally deserve it." I took a deep breath. "I was calling to tell you I'll be out of town for a while. I left last night, actually. A relative of mine in Seattle passed, my uncle. I need to help my cousins with the estate."

Sorrow colored her voice. "Oh, hon, I am so very sorry for your loss. You take as much time as you want, and let me know if you need anything." Her words took on a mother-hen tone. "I mean it. I know you've been saving, but do you have enough money?"

Fat tears rolled down my face, and I sniffled. "Yeah, I'll be all right. Thank you though, really. For everything."

"Come, now," she chided. "You'll be home soon. I'll even make that pie you like to celebrate. Just be sure to keep in touch, okay?"

Clearing my throat, I swiped my cheeks with the back of my hand. "Okay, sounds good. I'll miss you."

"I'll miss you too. Sometimes these things just happen. You stay safe up there, all right?"

"I will. Bye, Giselle."

"Bye, hon."

Blaze

He paced in the hallway while listening to her soft sniffles and one-sided conversation with his enhanced hearing. He felt strangely sympathetic for Sora. After centuries of ruling his Clutch and placing their interests above his own wellbeing, the emotion was oddly foreign.

Several times he stopped at the door with his hand hovering over the knob without realizing he had stopped at all.

He wanted to comfort her. That thought alone stayed his hand.

As he continued to pace, he only hoped she wouldn't hate him when he told her the truth…

Sora

My feet sank into the thick black carpet as I staggered to the attached bathroom. Trying to rub away the ache in my chest with one hand, I flipped the light on with the other. Shock coursed through me, and my mouth dropped open in awe. Wow, this bathroom was bigger than my entire studio.

A porcelain jacuzzi tub took up at least eight feet of space on one wall. The sounds of rushing water brought my eyes to the giant glass-enclosed shower with ten shower heads and… a waterfall inlaid with a mermaid-scaled mosaic pattern.

A waterfall… in the shower. I'd died and gone to heaven.

Panning the rest of the room, I noted the marble double vanity with reflective veins of silver running throughout the white stone. The lighting was excellent. Brushed nickel sconces lit the twelve-foot-high ceiling and drew the eye to the flecked travertine tile on the floor and walls.

Taking care of the insistent urge of my bladder in the separate powder room, I located my bag tucked into a corner below the light switch.

Hmm… turning on my heel, I locked the door. Where would the towels be? More importantly, which would be better: a nice long soak, or a shower under a waterfall…?

I opted for the waterfall. Yes…

Over an hour later, I stepped back into the bedroom with a bounce in my step.

Admiring my ensemble in the floor-length mirror, I fingered the holes of my band tee. Strategically placed, they bared my defined naval. My grey jeggings hugged every curve like a second skin and made my legs look even longer. I quickly plated my wet hair into a sloppy braid down my back while musing over the extraordinary shower. I could definitely get used to that bathroom.

A knock at the door drew my attention.

I hesitated. "Yes?"

The same man who delivered the succulent steak entered.

Quickly, I regarded his attire.

Pressed black Dockers paired with shiny dress shoes and a simple tucked-in white polo. He almost looked ready for a casual Friday at the office. I judged his age to be somewhere in the mid-forties. The creases at the corners of his brown eyes and thinning hair confirmed it. Pleasantly, he smiled. "Hello, miss. The Master has turned in for the day. Would you like a tour?"

My brows drew low. "Turned in?"

"Yes, to sleep."

Slightly disappointed, I murmured, "Oh, right." Lifting my hand, I wiggled my fingers. "Sure. I'm Sora, by the way."

He bowed once. "Julian, Head of the House. Pleased to meet you."

I grinned at the pomp and circumstance. "Likewise."

Gesturing to the hall with a flourish, he said, "This way, please."

Could this get any crazier? Smirking like a maniac, I followed him out.

Evidently it could.

This place was huge. At least six floors of towering stairs, two kitchens, plus a rec room complete with a bar and pool table. The formal dining room could seat over thirty people.

My mouth gaped as we stopped at the entertainment room. A giant projector took up one wall opposite multiple overstuffed leather reclining chairs and tables.

They even had an indoor infinity pool. The water ended with a glass wall that showcased an underwater view into a well-manicured courtyard complete with topiaries. The birds of paradise were in full bloom. Their orange petals were completely open inside their mock avian beaks.

This was the only place in the entire house I'd seen sunlight. Glancing up, I noted a steel retractable roof.

Bewildered, I wondered just how loaded Blaze was.

Curious, I turned toward Julian as he stood just inside the doorway. "Are you not a Vampire, then?"

He chortled, "No, Miss Sora. I'm human and am a part of the Menagerie Master Blaze employs here. I take care of the day-to-day things."

My cheeks reddened. "Uh, sorry about that. This is all very new to me."

Eyes softening in compassion, he nodded. "It's quite all right. I can imagine the shock of it all. I was born into this role. In fact, generations of my family have served Master Blaze."

Shocked, my voice quivered. "Generations..."

If he noticed the question in my eyes, he ignored it. Turning, he tipped his head back the way we'd come. "Would you like a snack? Perhaps a drink service in the library?"

My brows rose. "Library?" Maybe I could get some answers there.

"Of course, we have everything one could need here. Right this way." His shoes whispered on the endless black carpet as he left me to follow.

I don't think I would classify it as a library. It was more like a museum of rare books.

The rows extended beyond my vision with lighted cases sporadically butting up against the tall stacks. Plush chairs were strategically placed near nickel lamps at varying intervals. A genuine crystal chandelier hung roughly thirty feet overhead at the center of a tinted, dome glass ceiling.

Noting my gaze, Julian tilted his chin upward. "It's strong enough to keep out ninety-eight percent of UVA and UVB light."

"Impressive. I've never seen a tinted bubble before."

He smiled. "Quite. Well I must be off. Are you sure you don't need anything else?"

My cheeks flushed. "Of course! I didn't mean to keep you. Um, just one more thing: I haven't seen another soul." I stammered, "Is, um, everyone… asleep?"

Cocking his head, he silently evaluated me. "Most of the Menagerie keeps the same hours as Master Blaze."

He didn't mention any other Vampires, and that was the second time he'd said *Menagerie*. What the hell was that? Keeping my curiosity to myself, I nodded. "Oh. Okay. Sorry for keeping you for so long."

"Nonsense, it was my pleasure." He hesitated. "I trust you can get back to your room on your own?"

Definitely not. I lied, "Of course! Thank you."

With another small bow, he left.

I wandered around for a good fifteen minutes before finding anything noteworthy.

Yes! An entire section on magic. Perusing the stack, I looked for a rhyme or reason to the organization. It seemed to be divided by the type of magic…

Blood Magic

Water Magic

Memoirs of a Fire Mage

Defensive Magic

I kept skimming the titles before finally finding what I was searching for.

Warding

Excited, I grabbed the thick tome, relaxed into a cushy chair, and tucked my legs beneath me.

The book was well over a hundred years old. Its spine was bound with a thick leather cord. Gently, I ran my fingertips over the tooled cover. With a shaking hand, I opened the tome. Yellow with age, the vellum showcased cramped cursive, complete with whorls and flourishes popular during the period. Thank the Goddess it was English. I began at the beginning…

By the third book, I was beyond frustrated. Every single page spoke of spellcasting, circles, ingredients to imbue a portable ward, but nothing on what I had done with my magic.

Standing, I stomped out the pins and needles in my legs.

Skimming the titles once more, I settled on *Defensive Magic* and hoped there would be something useful inside.

Blaze

Rising at dusk, he didn't immediately recognize his surroundings.

As I took in a quick breath of air, everything came rushing back.

Sora…

Quickly dressing, he began following her unique, delicate fragrance.

Her scent crisscrossed all throughout the mansion.

Stopping at his personal suite, he knocked. No sounds of movement met his ears.

She'd obviously taken the tour with Julian. Perhaps he should check in with his Head of the House first.

Zipping through the multiple hallways and flights of stairs at Vampiric speed, he quickly arrived in the kitchen.

Anxiety to find the woman in question colored his words. Briskly, he barked, "Julian, report."

Julian bowed. "Good evening, Master. All is well." Smiling thoughtfully, he interpreted his Master's objective. "I left Miss Sora reading in the library." Lifting his wrist, he checked the time. His eyes widened. "Several hours ago. Has she not returned to your suite?"

Blaze barely heard the last word before he flashed away with his mind swirling. In his haste to get her settled, and with his strength sapped by the dawn, he had forgotten to issue the order that she was *not* a part of the Menagerie...

She had better be safe.

Sora

The feeling of being watched jerked me awake.

A tall man loomed before me. The book I'd been reading hit the floor with a dull thud. Gripping the leather chair, I choked out, "Who are you?"

He inhaled. "Jackson. My, my, don't you smell delicious." Grinning, he flashed two sharp canines against his lower lip.

Vampire, my mind screeched. Time slowed. "Stop."

Jackson's eyes glazed over as he froze with the tip of his tongue touching one fang.

I stood, and my heart slowed to a calmer rate. Slowly, I circled him.

Dirty blond, his hair was cropped close in a military cut. The color of his irises was nearly black with hunger. High cheekbones paired with a thinner jaw... He looked just like... Blaze. Strong, commanding, and corded in the same thick muscle, but shorter. Almost identical in their attire, except this Vampire wore a hunter-green T-shirt.

Returning to perch on the edge of my chair, I pushed my will. "What do you want?"

Without missing a beat, his tongue slipped back into his mouth. "To taste you."

He stated it so nonchalantly, I shuddered. I was NOT chattel.

Glaring, I confidently ordered, "I am NOT food. You will respect me. You will forget your hunger for me."

"I will respect you," he parroted in a monotone. "You are not food. I will no longer seek your blood."

Satisfied, I nodded. "Go."

He was there one moment and gone the next.

Blaze instantly appeared. His eyes flashed black as he growled, "We need to talk." Turning, he strode away.

I scrambled after him, as his long legs quickly outpaced mine.

What the hell did I do now? He was going to bite me! Me! What does *he* have to be so pissed off about?

By the time we reached the interior of my, er *his*, room, I was furious.

"What?" I half yelled, kicking the door closed with one heel. No way was I going to sit on the bed for one of his mood swings.

He paced, his muscular legs making short work of the large room. "You," he whispered. "You lied to me!"

Defiantly, I jutted out my chin. "About what?"

Abruptly, he stopped at the wall. "You compelled my Trackers… and my brother."

"So what?" I spat. "He wanted to EAT ME!"

His shoulders slumped. Sighing in defeat, he rumbled, "It's my fault. I should have told the Clutch you were off-limits." Staring at the floor, he uttered, "I'm sorry."

I was taken aback, and my mind stuttered at the flip of his emotions. I expected a fight, and yet… he was apologizing. Studying his stance, I tucked my chin. "It's okay, we both have our secrets."

He fell onto the wingback. Rubbing his face with one massive hand, he ran his fingers through his hair.

As I watched the blond strands settle, I had an overwhelming urge to touch it. Focus!

My Chucks sank into the carpet as I strode to the edge of the bed to face him. "Where should we start?"

His eyes roamed my face. "I need a promise from you first."

Suspicious, my brows lowered. "A promise. What kind of promise?"

He leaned back, his gaze drifting to the white ceiling. In a factual tone, he stated, "Your magic is new. I have some things to tell you, but I don't want to be fried to a crisp by any outburst of your power. My Clutch needs to be kept safe. Can you promise to keep a level head?"

I waited a beat and answered honestly. "I'm not sure. I guess it would depend on what you have to tell me. I can promise to try though."

Jerking his head, he seemed to come to a decision. "Okay. I'll start with what my research revealed. I placed several calls while you were sleeping last night, to ferret out secrets from the Seattle Clutch. Individual Clutches are extremely territorial and don't share lightly. About twenty-three years ago, their previous Master went mad. He had just passed his first millennium."

Appalled by the thought of a millennia-old mad Vampire, I interrupted, "How old are you?"

"That's not important, just listen. His erratic behavior gained the notice of Seattle's Magic Council. They in turn deployed two of their most powerful Mages to make an example of him. There was a massive battle near the shore of an unpopulated stretch of Oak Harbor. Both Mages were badly injured, but managed to circle him inside a ward. Using his blood on their weapons mixed with their own, they summoned dire-fire and burned him alive."

He paused.

I knew of dire-fire from my many tutors as a teen. It could only be summoned by the strongest Mages, and only with Blood Magic. Nothing could survive it. The soil where it was used would be fallow for decades. I answered his unspoken question: "Yes."

Making a noise of approval, he continued, "The Mages survived. From what I gathered, there was a male and female. The female was pregnant. Eight months later, she birthed a healthy baby girl."

I waited.

Sighing heavily, he spelled it out for me: "I think that baby was you."

What? No way. My parents were powerful, sure, but I would remember a story like that. Clenching my lids, I tried to remember something, anything from my buried past.

A single memory came forth. I was maybe four or five. My mother was teaching me how to swim. She wore a red swimsuit, and I had asked her about a scar on her left shoulder. She said it was just an old wound.

Seeing it in my mind's eye, I deduced now what my young self could not. Two ragged parallel lines marred her perfect skin. They hadn't healed properly and had left a four-inch scar. Two fang marks…

Coming back to the moment, I quipped, "So?"

Noting my acknowledgment, he continued, "As Vampires age, they gain power. That is why there is a Master in each Clutch. We police our own with that power, and gain it from our Clutch in return. I really don't know what happened with whatever injury your mother sustained, but Vampire venom is incredibly toxic. Lethal even, if the Vampire chooses it to be. If she was bitten, combined with her own power and that of a growing child, I don't know what the outcome would be. There are too many variables to be certain, but I think that bite, while you were in utero, transferred something to you."

"And you think I am this child. I didn't even have magic until a few days ago." Chuckling, I dismissed his words. "What you're saying makes no sense."

Guiltily, he added, "There's more."

My hackles rose at the look in his eyes. I threw my hands up in an "out with it" gesture.

Standing in one smooth motion, he stepped closer to the door. "That night at Curley's, yes?"

I nodded.

"I could smell a touch of Vampire. As I left, I brushed against you to gather your scent. Curious, I waited until you left, and followed you from a distance. I'm not sure exactly how I lost control, but one moment I was a block from you, the next my fangs were in your neck and you were sprawled on the ground."

I balled my fists on the mattress, and he held his hands placatingly. "I sealed the wounds and moved you to the grass. I was confused, and euphoric with the taste of you. I have never tasted anything so sweet in all my years. Your blood called to me. It was all I could do to resist. I had to leave you. I couldn't risk losing myself to the bloodlust and injuring you further. I think my bite activated something in you on a cellular level, something dormant. You can control Vampires, something only a Master can do. You even smell like we do."

My clenched fists lit. The blue flames licked up my arms. My braid glowed liquid silver in the flickering light. Standing, I faced him. "You. You're the reason for all of this! You left me there?" My flames grew larger by the moment as my face turned red in anger. "I was robbed! I could have died! YOU HURT AND LEFT ME?"

He stepped toward me. "Calm down. I honestly didn't mean to hurt you."

I put a hand out to stop him from coming closer. Vivid azure light shot from my outstretched palm and raced toward him. He barely flashed out of the way before it hit the door where he'd been. Instantly, it ignited.

Stunned, the fire on my hands winked out. Mesmerized, I watched the white flames lick at the wood paneling.

Blaze

That was too close, he thought, rushing into the bathroom to unlatch the fire extinguisher underneath the sink.

Zipping back to the bedroom door, he pulled the pin and sprayed the growing flames.

FUCK! It was dire-fire!

Dropping the canister, he turned to Sora. Gently, he grasped her shoulders and shook her. "Sora. Sora!" It wasn't working! Taking her delicate face in his large hands, he did the only thing he thought might work.

He kissed her. Softly, he murmured against her mouth, "Sora."

Life returned to her vacant form. Beautiful sapphire eyes flecked with silver, like the bioluminescence of sea life deep below the ocean's surface, stared back at him.

Lifting his other hand, he placed his palm between her breasts where the center of her magic lay. "Call it back, Love. Call the flames back to you."

Sora

Staring into the depths of his anguished cobalt eyes, I slowly came back to myself.

"Sora, please," he begged.

Seeing me finally focus, he stepped behind me and gripped my shoulders.

I cried out in shock at the destruction of my power. "I don't know how!"

Seeking more fuel, the flames crawled over the door frame.

He leaned down, and his breath tickled my neck. "Shh. It will be okay. Just touch it. Your body will know what to do."

My Chucks felt like leaden weights as I stumbled forward with Blaze's reassuring presence at my back. Reaching out, I expected to be burned, but wasn't. It felt like warm bath water to my splayed fingertips. The flames licked and bumped against my hand like a playful puppy.

It was alive.

Feeling the echo of it in my chest, I called it back. The tendrils receded from the wall first, then the frame. Lingering on the door, they begged to stay. Tethering it to my center, I tugged harder. As it reconnected with my well, I leaned against Blaze with a relieved sigh.

Everything was untouched, as if my fire had never burned at all.

My thoughts tripped. He could have been killed. I was a monster.

His lips brushed the shell of my ear. "That's my girl."

I no longer had the energy to fight. Turning out of his arms, I walked to the bed and curled into a ball. Tears hit the pillow, leaving dark splotches where they landed. "Just leave me alone."

As the latch clicked, I cried myself to sleep.

Janelle Peel

Chapter 5

Blaze

He waited outside the door until her cries quieted and her breathing evened out.

What was he going to do? She probably despised him now. The look of hurt on her face when he admitted his guilt…

Shaking himself, he vowed he would win her over. She was a rare gem, one he couldn't let anyone else have. Her power alone marked her as a threat to the entire supernatural world. She would be systematically broken down and abused if caught; bent toward someone else's will or worse; killed.

Even her own people would covet her power.

He refused to allow it. She was his Firestarter…

Sora

Rolling over, I languidly stretched. Reaching to the side table for my phone, I checked the time. It'd been a couple hours.

Padding to the bathroom to take care of the necessities, I pondered my power and the harm it could cause. Shooting fire when my emotions got the best of me wasn't an option. I needed practice.

Thank the Goddess Blaze wasn't hurt. Although it wouldn't have been a bad idea to singe him a bit. After all, this crap started with him.

My mind rebelled at placing all the blame squarely at his feet. True, I wasn't exactly being fair. Sure, if he'd have kept his damned fangs to himself, I might have lived for a while longer in my bland little bubble.

If he really sniffed me out at the bar, it was probably only a matter of time before someone or something else would have too.

Was this why I hadn't been eating? The only thing that tasted good at all was rare, bloody meat. I had to get more answers.

Splashing water onto my face, I tugged out my braid. Finger-combing the tresses, I froze.

He'd kissed me.

During my entire pity party, I had forgotten the kiss. Just a brush of his lips… I traced where his had been, and they tingled with the remembered sensation. Was it to shock me back into the present? Did it mean anything? I replayed the moment in my mind. "Call it back, Love. Call the flames back to you." He'd called me *love*. What did that mean?

There was one thing I could actually do something about. I was starving.

After a detour for some food, I would hunt down everything related to magic.

The sound of dishes clacked in my ears as I approached the smaller of the two kitchens. As I hesitated at the door, the smells of cooked meat swirled through the air. Savoring the aroma, I pushed through the swinging panel.

Julian stood front and center, seemingly aware of every task the two women were undertaking.

He addressed a short female with cropped hair chopping something green. "Georgia, no. You must dice the celery to achieve the proper texture."

Sauntering over to Georgia, a heavy-set woman with a brown bun pulled the knife from her grasp. "Like this."

Julian nodded. "Yes." Noticing me, he turned with a half bow. "Ah, Miss Sora. What can we do for you?"

My lashes fluttered. "Hey, Julian. Just Sora, please."

"As you wish."

Hopefully, I asked, "Um, do you have any more of that delicious ribeye from earlier?"

Without taking his gaze from mine, he smiled. "Julie, could you be a dear and grab the rare steak you just finished searing?"

Julie quickly pulled open the oven. Using a towel, she removed a steaming plated steak and handed it to him.

He tipped his head graciously. "Thank you."

"Miss, er, hmm," he stuttered, grabbing a tray setting off the sideboard, "Sora, would you like to take this in the formal dining room?"

Janelle Peel

Blushing, I pointed to a stainless-steel bar with two matching wooden stools just out of the way of the chefs. "Um, could I take it at that spot over there?"

He paused for a moment. "Of course."

Judging by his reaction, this definitely wasn't the norm for guests. My brows lifted. "Are you sure?" I didn't want to get him into trouble.

"Yes, yes. Absolutely fine. Would you care for a drink? Wine, perhaps?"

Hungry as I was, I didn't want to risk any alcohol. "Yes, please. Ice water is fine, thank you."

As I perched on the stool, the kitchen continued to bustle around me. Julian placed the setting in front of me, and I almost swooned at the sight. Cutting off a bite, I noted its red juicy perfection. Popping it into my mouth, I sighed. Pure Heaven. I barely noticed the water as he set it beside my elbow.

Using the last few morsels to soak up as much blood as I could, I pushed the plate away. Goddess, that was simply amazing.

Georgia snatched the plate up on her way to the dishwashing station.

I called after her, "Thank you."

A bob of her head was the only acknowledgement I received.

Okay…

As I hopped up, the kitchen was strangely empty. Shrugging, I made my way to the library.

I had gone through ten more tomes before he appeared.

Hesitating at the end of the closest stack, he rumbled, "Hey."

Throwing him a frustrated glare, I snapped, "What?"

He stepped back at my tone.

"Sorry," I mumbled. "I'm just irritated. Nothing in these books even comes close to what I've done with my power." Tipping my head back onto the plush chair, I pinched the bridge of my nose. Peeking at him beneath a fan of lashes, I watched him stare at my exposed throat.

Gulping, he cleared his throat. "I could help, if you want. My manipulation of magic is different than yours, but I'm sure between the two of us, we can figure something out."

Smirking internally at his reaction, I nodded. "That would probably be best."

"Perhaps, we could go to the courtyard? It would be..." he paused as if choosing his words carefully "...less traumatic for my Menagerie."

Now the silence in the kitchen made sense. They had probably heard all about my near miss with their, I mentally air quoted, "Master."

Disappointed in myself and my own lack of information, I muttered, "Sure."

Navigating the hallways leading to the courtyard, I couldn't help but admire the view.

His black shitkickers made absolutely no sound. Defining the round globes of his flawless rear, the fabric of his faded jeans bunched and released with each step. The black tee he wore rippled, highlighting every muscle as his thickly corded arms swung with the momentum.

Why did he have to look like walking sin?

Focus!

Finally, we reached our destination. The blooms seemed to smell sweeter in the predawn hours.

Looking up at the slowly lightening sky, he rumbled, "We don't have much time."

Where were we, exactly? I could see each star, something not visible in PB due to San Diego's light pollution.

He shifted toward me, and his face was nearly indistinguishable in the gloom. "Light your fire."

Closing my eyes, I focused my attention on the well of energy inside my chest. A ping answered. I flipped my lids open, and my hands illuminated with flickering flames. Shadows danced along the foliage from their bright light.

"Good. Focus on the fire. Feel your magic, manipulate it. Use your will to cast an image into the air, anything you'd like to see."

Doing as he asked, I conjured an image of the beach. I could hear the roar of the waves cresting and slapping against each other. Palms swayed in the breeze. Children laughed as they happily played in the wet sand.

Blaze's sharp inhale drew my attention.

Like a motion picture drawn with the ember of a smoking campfire stick, every detail I imagined glowed with starlight. The children buried one another in the sand. A breeze swept through the courtyard, teasing my hair as it shook the palm fronds. Ocean waves crested with an audible crack of thunder somewhere in the distance.

Startled by the sound, the leash on my power slipped.

Water leapt from the infinity pool in a live wave, instantly soaking my Chucks. With the cool sensation seeping into my socks, I released the tether completely. The picture continued for a beat, paused, then snapped in a shower of sparkling fairy dust.

Slightly dizzy, I sat down. My grey jeggings soaked up the liquid like a sponge, and I didn't care. I did it! Excited, I grinned up to Blaze's hulking figure. "Like that?"

Mouth hanging open in awe, he turned. "I think that was a little different," he said, his thumb and forefinger pinched together, "than I imagined."

I giggled. "Me too, but super amazing, right?"

Staring where the image had been, he questioned, "Was it a memory?"

The smile slid off my face. "Yes. I saw it from my hotel window in Cancun. My family had business there. I was stuck inside reading about magic I didn't have. It looked like so much fun to just play in the surf."

Thunder crackled again overhead as the cloudy sky opened. Rain began to pour, further soaking us.

Walking over to a switch on the wall, Blaze closed the retractable roof. "How do you feel?"

Listening to the soft whir of the motor, I took inventory. Other than the quickly passing dizziness, I felt good. Giddy even.

"I was dizzy, but now I feel great."

As the metal plates closed, Blaze squished his way over and sat beside me. "That's good. You ate before though, right?"

"Yes."

"Your magic needs fuel, or it will use your body as a source. Have you—" he paused "—had any strange cravings?"

Blushing, I tucked my chin and hid behind the curtain of my damp hair. "Yes. Nothing tastes right. The only thing I seem to crave is rare meat."

Reaching out, he tucked my tresses behind one ear. He traced the curve of my jaw with his thumb, and his eyes sparkled like sapphire gems in the near darkness. "It's okay." Expression shuttering, he dropped his hand. "I think you need blood."

My mouth opened in repulsion.

Jerking his head, he rushed out, "I think you're some kind of hybrid. A Mage and a Dhampir. It makes sense if your powers are tied to certain cravings. It's not so bad, really. If you're not ready, we can try other things." Earnestly, he added, "Keep it in mind, please?"

Gross… but if he was right… I nodded. "Okay. What now?"

Listening to the rain hit the steel roof, he sighed. "Well, obviously you have an affinity for weather. A thunderstorm wasn't forecasted."

I laughed, then guffawed.

His wide shoulders shook. Was he having fun too? A loud snort from his direction confirmed it.

Teasingly, I whispered, "Nice."

He sobered. "Water as well, judging by my half-drained pool. I felt the breeze also."

"So that leaves Earth, right?"

"Yes. I think we should try for that tomorrow night though," he chuckled. "I don't want to take a mud bath."

I sniggered. "Afraid of some dirt?"

"No. I don't want to push you too hard, too fast." His tone lowered. "We need to talk about something."

Reluctantly, the grin slid off my face. I was actually enjoying the banter; it felt good. "What now?"

Eyeing me, he stated in a factual tone, "I've never seen what you have done so far. Fire, Water, weather, and Air. Even now you are incredibly powerful. Like a mini sun, I can sense your well of magic as it calls to my own. You can control Vampires, something only a Master can do. These things alone will make you highly sought after. If you can also control Earth, there won't be a limit to what you can do. I've also never seen a Mage wield magic like you. They use spells, rituals, and the like. You would be the ultimate weapon."

His words slowly sunk in as my good mood soured. A weapon? The way I wield magic from my well? The questions swirled through my mind in an unending loop. "If I'm a weapon, what do you want out of this?"

Open and honest, he met my gaze. "I am partially responsible for your state. Had I not attacked you, this may never have happened. To make amends for my acts, I want to help you. Once you can defend yourself, you can do as you wish. Until that time, you are vulnerable. The Pack already has your scent. It's not safe for you to be anywhere else."

I debated the sincerity of his words for a moment. He had helped me so far, albeit in a creepy way. Then he'd given me a haven from the Shifters after my warding accident... He seemed genuine. Plus, he hadn't intentionally harmed me since he lost control after the bar. The strange looks from almost every human I encountered since his bite flitted past. "What happened to my scent when you bit me? All the humans, except for Giselle and my friend, got a bit weird. Some just stared; others made googly eyes. I even got a few dirty looks from a couple of women."

"It's the pheromones. Vampires have an innate ability in their scent." He paused. "It puts most humans into what we call *thrall*, and it makes them easier to compel." Lifting a finger at my horrified expression, he continued, "Let me finish. New Vampires learn to control it fairly early after being turned. Giselle and your friend are probably immune to your pheromones because they've been near you for so long."

I pondered that for a moment. "So, I can control it?"

His shoulder lifted. "Yes, with a bit of practice it should fade."

"Why aren't Julian or the kitchen staff affected?"

"Practice. They live with Vampires. We can't hold someone in thrall indefinitely." He stood. "It's mainly used to help us feed."

My nose wrinkled. Man, the hits just kept on coming.

Shaking my head, I pushed off the muddy ground and stepped beside him. Dusting chunks of mud and grass off my ass, I made my decision. "I will stay, for a while." Somberly, I added, "I don't have anywhere else to go anyway."

His face softened. "I'm so sorry, Sora."

Lifting a shoulder into a half shrug, I squished my way to the door. "I figure it probably would have happened sooner or later. Then, I'd probably be dead."

Blaze

As she walked back into the house, he shuddered. Thinking of her dead left him feeling ill.

He quickly caught up to her in the hall as she headed back to her room.

Curiously, she asked, "Where do you sleep?"

Slowing his pace, he watched the sway of her silver hair as it waved against her back. "On the main floor since you took over my suite."

He smirked at the thought of her in his bed.

"Ha, funny," she snarked.

Furrowing his brows, he asked, "Would you like a different room?"

Hand on the handle, she turned with an incredulous expression. "Are you kidding? That shower is the best thing on Earth." She stuck out her tongue. "This room is now mine, buddy." She chuckled, but then the playfulness went out of her eyes.

His hackles rose. "What is it?"

"Well, um," she murmured. Blushing, she waved down the corridor. "I was wondering, could you stay in a room up here?"

Ah. Yes, a new house full of strangers would be hard for her. Especially after her encounter with his brother. He should have thought of that sooner. Nodding, he lifted his arm to the door beside hers. "As you wish. I'll be just there. Rest well, Sora."

"You too." She smiled and closed the door.

Pleased that she felt more comfortable with him near, he went off in search of Julian to move his accommodations.

Blaze found him in the pantry taking inventory.

At his approach, Julian paused.

Bowing once, he straightened. "Yes, Master Blaze. What might I assist you with?"

"Good morning, Julian. I need one of the Menagerie to move my accommodations to the room beside Sora's."

Nodding, he smiled. "Ah, yes. It will be done. How is Miss Sora settling in?"

"Better, it seems. She is magnificent. Her powers might even exceed my own." Boyishly, he grinned. "I hope she stays."

Julian's eyes sparkled. "We will do all we can to make her feel welcome. I will have your room ready within the hour. Will there be anything else? Sustenance, perhaps?"

His stomach rolled at the thought of taking any vein other than Sora's "No, that's fine. Thank you, Julian."

"Of course, Master." Issuing another half bow, Julian reached for his phone.

Satisfied, Blaze zipped to the rec room for a drink.

Approaching the bar, he snagged a bottle of whiskey when his brother arrived through the side hallway. His large hand tightened on the neck so hard it almost cracked. *Mine*, his mind screamed.

Snatching a rocks glass, he tried for a neutral tone as he poured. "Jackson."

Jackson smirked. "Blaze."

Remembering Sora's commands to respect her, he decided a test was in order. Taking a sip, he inquired, "So, have you met Sora?"

Jackson's eyes glazed over. "Yes, she's a very nice girl."

He baited, "Yes, she is. Have you noticed the delicate notes of her scent?"

Face scrunching in confusion, Jackson slowly replied, "No. I mean, she smelled pleasant."

Not wanting to push her compulsion too far, he eased off. "What are you up to so early in the morning?"

Jackson shrugged. "Just came in for a nightcap."

Grabbing another cup, he poured a few fingers. Sliding it across the polished oak, he asked, "How's the perimeter?"

Jackson squinted. "A few extra Shifters were scented, but nothing too abnormal."

Blaze's face turned to stone. They'd followed. Damn, he hoped he'd lost them. That was a foolhardy thought. A gift like Sora would definitely be worth pursuing for the Pack.

Mine, his mind whispered more insistently.

He drain his glass and then spoke, his voice sounding like tumbled stones. "Increase sentries, day and night. Move the majority of Feline Shifters to the day shift with the Protectors."

Jackson barely blinked. "Consider it done. Care to tell me why?"

Pouring another drink, Blaze debated on how much he could tell him. Jackson was his brother, best friend, and second in command. He'd also lusted after Sora's blood… then again, so had Blaze. Decision made, he knocked his knuckles on the bar for luck. "Sora—" he hesitated, knowing the words he spoke would cement what he had known all along "—she's a strong Mage, the strongest I've ever seen… and she's… my Mate."

Jackson barked a quick laugh. Looking at Blaze's deadpan expression, he immediately sobered. "You're serious, aren't you?" His eyes widened. "You are. Do you know how rare a female Vampire is?" Doubt colored his words. "Let alone to find one and have her be your Mate?"

"Yes," Blaze growled in disapproval, "I am aware."

"Wait. You said Mage. When did you have the time to turn her? I've never heard of a Vampire Mage."

Sighing, Blaze shook his head. This was the crux of it all. Looking Jackson straight in the eye, he lowered his voice. "I didn't. She's still in her first life. She's a Dhampir Mage Hybrid."

The words dropped like bombs in the quiet room.

Jackson's pupils dilated as his mouth opened and closed like a fish out of water.

Baring all his secrets, Blaze continued, "Her mother was bitten while she was in the womb by that psychotic Master Vampire in Seattle. Her parents are the most powerful Mages in the Supernatural

Community. Something happened, I don't know what." Waving his hands at the situation, he added, "Then I fed on her."

Jackson gasped.

Frustrated with himself, Blaze began whisper yelling. "I lost control, Jackson! I haven't done that since I was a Fledgling!" Taking a deep breath, he calmed. "My venom awoke her powers. She had none beforehand."

Understanding dawned on Jackson's face. "Who else knows this?"

Worry creased lines into the shape of a *v* between Blaze's brows. "A Shifter caught her scent. He visited her home."

A deranged laugh escaped him as he filled Jackson in on the charred Wolf flying from Sora's landing and skidding through the grass.

Jackson sniggered. "So, you brought her home?"

"She called me. An accident, she said. Regardless, the fool shouldn't have tried to enter her home. I believe he was testing her powers and literally bit off more than he could chew."

Jackson was a quick study. His expression lit with suspicion. "What are you leaving out? How did she have your number?"

Blaze wasn't prepared to air all of Sora's secrets. He didn't want his Clutch to know she also exhibited a Master's powers, and label her as a threat. It was a delicate balance, swearing fealty to another Vampire. He'd never had to place a compulsion on any member of his Clutch, and hoped to keep it that way. In a tone that brooked no argument, he replied, "It's not relevant to the matter at hand."

"Okaaay," Jackson drew out with a shrug. "What happened next?"

"It was close." Blaze ran his hands through his hair. "Once she told me the Wolf was Mel, I convinced her of the danger and made her pack a bag."

"Mel. Mel, the Alpha Mel?" Jackson asked, flabbergasted.

"Yes. Sora wouldn't leave without making sure the woman who had taken her in was safe." He threw his arms wide open. "She made a type of ward I have never seen, without uttering a single word. It covered an unattached garage, the yard, and a two-story home." Dropping his arms, he continued in an awed voice, "She was glorious."

Jackson snapped his fingers and waved his hand in a hurry-up gesture.

Gravely, Blaze continued, "The expenditure of power overtaxed her body and caused her to collapse. As I settled her and her belongings in my arms, I heard the first yip. It seems Mel really wanted her. I parsed no less than twenty scents as I zigzagged through Pacific Beach for over an hour to lose them." Pouring another shot, he quickly downed it before lifting his arm in a sweeping gesture. "Here we are."

Jackson gulped his drink and set the empty glass on the bar. "Here we are." Stuffing his hands inside his pockets, he turned toward the entryway. "Seems I have a while yet before I can rest. I'll have a full report compiled by this evening." Unimpressed with the situation, he clomped his boots through the hallway.

Alone with his thoughts, Blaze mentally went through the security of his compound. The Feline Shifters were excellent guards. Taking them into his Clutch had been one of his better decisions. He still couldn't believe Mel refused to let them join his Pack. Then again, the old adage of cats and dogs rang true.

The Protectors were also exceptional day guards. By regularly drinking Vampire blood, they were far stronger and faster than any normal human. They trained with military-like precision and were more familiar with technological security than any other member of his Clutch.

Mind swirling with scenarios, he made his way to back to the second floor to sleep.

'

Chapter 6

Jackson

As Jackson trudged down the underground tunnel to the Protector's barracks, his feet dragged against the rough cement floor. Usually, he moved through the reinforced steel tunnels as quickly as possible. Not today. *Day*, he thought, being the main part of that word.

Shaking his head, he wondered for the millionth time what it would be like to be Blaze. In control of every situation, more powerful than he, and more handsome. The few females he'd had over the decades had cruelly informed him so as they turned from his advances.

Then to find this Sora, his *Mate*. Sighing internally, Jackson couldn't help but think his selfish thoughts. Blaze had bested him, again. Jackson was the older brother. He was turned first after their parents passed with fever. Christ, he'd even supported Blaze until his twenty-fifth year when he was old enough to begin his second life.

Jackson loved his younger brother; dearly, in fact. However, things never seemed fair enough for his liking.

He threw his pity party for the few remaining minutes it took him to walk the length of the tunnel at human speed. If he was truly honest with himself, he wouldn't want to have Blaze's responsibility. A Clutch was a lot of work, work that he'd been happy to do without as second in command. Add in a Dhampir, the holy grail of Vampires, as a Mate? PLUS, the Mage aspect? No thank you.

As he warred with himself to make the best of the hand he was dealt, he arrived at the bunker. Turning the handle, he opened the heavy steel door. "Mason!"

Quick footsteps sounded on the metal rungs descending from the tube leading above ground. Almost as fast as a Vampire, Mason closed the distance across the underground chamber.

Snapping to attention, he barked, "Yes, sir!"

At six foot, Mason's wiry frame cut a trim figure beneath his fatigues. Short raven hair, trimmed to the same military style of Jackson's, suited his proficient personality. Bright blue eyes peered from above a narrow nose and square jaw.

Moving to sit on the black powder-coated bench, he growled, "Report on the Pack's movements."

Briskly, Mason answered, "Sir, so far they have been erratic. Three Shifters have tested the ward and have been successfully repelled at varying times throughout the night. Bear, Dingo, and Wolf."

"Was the Wolf missing any fur?"

"Yes, sir. A large brown Wolf was reported with a bald patch on his left foreleg."

Propping his ankle on the opposing knee, Jackson sighed. "We have a situation with the Shifters. All perimeter activity is to be reported to me immediately. Protectors and Shifters are to pair and parole the perimeter at fifteen-minute intervals during the day, with multiple sweeps interlaced along the fence line. I want a roving pair doing sporadic checks. I trust your opinion on how often." He rubbed his chin. "We may have a war with the Pack." Getting to his feet once more, he rumbled, "Dismissed."

With a snap of his heel, Mason nodded. "Sir!"

As Jackson closed the steel door and flashed down the tunnel, he couldn't help but wonder if war truly was on the horizon.

Sora

After some sleep, and a lengthy rain shower with lavender soap, I pondered what to wear. The thought of seeing Blaze made my stomach flip. I wanted to look my best.

Maybe the new-to-me off-the-shoulder purple slouch tee that showed my navel, and favorite faded jeans, with strappy heels?

No, I'd only ever worn Chucks around him. Heels were definitely out.

Deciding on silver ballet flats, I quickly dressed. Stepping into the bathroom once more, I deftly wove my wet hair into a fishtail braid. Admiring my ensemble, I plucked the phone off the nightstand and went to the bedroom door. Pressing my ear to the crack, I listened. Hearing no sounds, I stepped out.

The hall was deserted. I checked the time: 5:30 p.m. Had the sun gone down yet? Should I knock? Did Blaze switch rooms like I'd asked?

My internal monologue caused me to miss his door opening.

"Hey," he rumbled.

Startled, I blushed furiously. "Hi. Um, I didn't know, what time you uh, rose for the day…"

Letting out a shock of laughter, he smirked. "I think you've seen too many movies. I dream and wake like everyone else. Perhaps you would like a crash course in Vampirism?"

Nodding, I peered up at his ever-changing blue eyes. His gaze, however, wasn't on mine. Roving my face, he skimmed the line of my neck and bare shoulder.

Fine, I thought. Two can play this game.

I returned his perusal with one of my own. The huge black combat boots adorning his feet led to dark-washed jeans that hugged his calves and thighs. His narrow hips showcased the taut muscles of his abs, clearly visible from his painted-on sky-blue tee. Well-defined pecs rounded to the thickly corded muscles of his shoulders. His strong jaw had a slight sprinkling of stubble that met towel-dried, wet blond hair the color of honey. My mind halted, towel dried? The thought of Blaze in a towel sent my blood racing with heat. Mmm…

Inhaling deeply, he propped one massive arm above his head and leaned against the door frame. "See something you like?"

My eyes traced the thick blue veins standing out in sharp relief against his skin. Yummy. Of its own accord, my tongue slipped out to wet my lips. I was starving.

Shocked out of staring by the reason for my sudden hunger, I stepped back. Hiding behind my fanned lashes, I stammered, "Would you like to eat me?" My eyes widened. "Um, I mean, with me. *With* me. Would you like to go *with* me to eat?"

Grinning like a fool, he closed the door and flipped out a meaty hand. "After you."

Thankful for the chance to turn away, I hurried down the hall.

Oh my Goddess, did I really just say that? I have got to get it together!

Mortified, I didn't even notice our arrival at the kitchen until Blaze snagged my wrist. "Did you see that?"

Glancing back, I looked around. "See what?"

His fingers slid down to hold my hand. Leaning down to my exposed ear, he whispered, "How fast you moved."

Distracted by his warm breath on my skin, it took a moment to process his words. My face screwed up. Moved? I whispered back, "What are you talking about?"

At the sound of dishes scraping and a murmur of voices, Blaze released his grip. He pushed on the swinging door, his voice taking on a normal tone. "Never mind. We'll talk about it later."

Flexing my hand, I followed him inside.

The same stainless steel greeted my eyes when I entered the bustling kitchen. Julian immediately came forward from his post while tapping a clipboard with his pen. Half bowing, he said, "Good evening, Master Blaze, Miss Sora."

I beamed. "Just Sora, please."

"Yes, yes, Sora. Can I get you anything? Another steak, perhaps?"

Suddenly, I wasn't hungry at all. Strange, I'd been starving a few moments before. I was thirsty though. Hopping onto a bar stool, I nodded. "Just a bottle of water, please."

Blaze appeared at my elbow with a disapproving look. "You need to eat if we are to practice magic tonight."

Raising a brow, I quipped, "I'm not hungry right now. I'll be fine."

Julian arrived with a bottle and placed it on the counter. "Will there be anything else, Sora?"

Pleased that he had now dropped the Miss, I smiled. "No thank you, Julian. This is fine."

He turned toward Blaze's frowning form. "Master Blaze?"

Shaking his head, he addressed Julian dismissively. "No, I believe we will be on our way." Touching my shoulder, he jerked his head back the way we'd come.

Julian issued his half bow once more as we exited.

Glaring at the broody Vampire, I snapped, "What was that all about?"

His face was glacial. "You need to eat."

I barked a laugh. "Are you my mother now? I'm a grown-ass woman, Blaze; I'll eat when I'm hungry." Jerk. What was his problem anyway? Oh, looks like the Master didn't get his way and is having a fit. The corner of my mouth lifted as I stuck out my tongue.

Unscrewing the cap of my water, I took a sip. "Where are we going?"

He growled, "The courtyard."

Okaaaaay, this should be fun—not. I sighed. One moment he was all smiles and sexual innuendo, the next he was like a marble statue. Hopefully, the night would improve.

Walking by the indoor infinity pool, a breeze rustled the small hairs on the back of my neck. As I glanced over for the origin, Jackson appeared seemingly out of thin air. I squeaked in surprise.

Instantly, I was behind Blaze's large body and blocked entirely from view.

"What did you do?" Blaze rumbled.

Jackson threw his hands up in surrender and took a step back. "Nothing. I came to report on the security of the perimeter." Sarcastically, he added, "Like you asked."

I peeked around one toned bicep. Jackson's gaze skipped to mine in silent question.

A loud growl filled my ears. Turning around, I began searching for the source. Nothing was there. Stepping around Blaze's massive form, I looked at Jackson, and the rumble increased. My heart rate soared through the roof as fight-or-flight adrenaline lit my veins. My azure flames appeared, called by my instinctual reaction to whatever threat there was.

Jackson studied the floor intensely. Slyly, he made a pointing gesture from his hip toward his brother.

Confused, I followed the line of his finger. Menace radiated from every line of Blaze's body as different portions of him flickered in and out with the glow of my fire. Stepping closer to his massive frame, the rumbling lowered in volume. Bravely, I placed my glimmering palm on the center of his chest. It vibrated for a moment more, then stilled.

The source of the sound was him… *growling.*

I replayed the scene in my mind for the cause. He was in front of me, then Jackson came, I squeaked, and Blaze was instantly between us.

As if... he was *protecting* me.

Jackson let out an audible sigh from behind me. I glanced at him over my shoulder.

Shrugging, he met my eyes.

Blaze's chest started to rumble again, and Jackson immediately dropped his gaze. The growl gained in intensity as I tested my theory and stared at Jackson. Moving my hand up the swell of Blaze's pecs, I traced his bulging jugular. The growl cut off completely and he made a different noise…

He *purred*.

Shocked, I dropped my hand.

Slowly relaxing, the hard lines of Blaze's body softened.

"Sooooo," I drew out, extinguishing my flames. "That was interesting."

Clearing his throat, Blaze grumbled, "Sorry."

Face glued to the marble, Jackson nodded. "Just text me when you want the report."

I blinked, and he was gone. How the hell did they move so fast? Shelving the thought, I bypassed Blaze to the courtyard. Sitting on a stone bench, I lifted a brow. "I'm guessing we need to have that Vampire talk now?"

He followed and sat quietly next to me.

Bumping him with my shoulder, I pressed, "Care to explain that?"

Staring straight ahead, he replied in a tired tone, "That was a Vampire instinct."

Placing my water on the ground, I mumbled, "Uh huh."

"It was a protective reaction. You sounded frightened, and I overreacted." He bumped my shoulder back. "I apologize if I scared you."

Deciding to let it drop, I went with an easier topic. "So, tell me about Vampires in general. I grew up knowing about different supernaturals, but have no knowledge beyond the fact of their existence."

He let out a relieved breath. "I'll start at the beginning. Only Masters can create new Vampires. Even then they only turn one or two per decade. It's a large drain on their power and time. *Fledglings* is what new Vampires are called. The Clutch helps the transition from human to Vampire, but it can be very difficult. The bloodlust is incredibly hard to overcome, and it can take weeks to years depending on the will of each individual. During the bloodlust period, we are little more than animals and are guided by the need for blood. Fledglings are constantly supervised and are never allowed human contact until they can master their urges. Only then does the Fledgling start to remember who they are, and is welcome to interact with the Menagerie."

"How do they feed then, as," I tripped over the unfamiliar word, "Fledglings?"

"Members of the Menagerie donate blood. It's taken via IV. The Fledgling is given the bagged blood." He glanced over to see if I was following.

I nodded. "And the Menagerie are people that live within the Clutch?" My face screwed up. "Like slaves?"

He chuckled, "No. Most Menageries are made up of people on retainer. They are paid quite well. They live here, with us. More like servants, though most have tight bonds and are considered a part of our family. Take my Clutch for example. Julian has been with us since he was born. I knew his parents and theirs. Sure, we do take on new people, but it's very rare. They take care of the household. It's very similar to a small community."

"So, they get paid. Do they ever get to leave?"

"Yes. They go on vacations just like everyone else." A sculpted brow rose. "I don't force people to stay here, if that's what you're asking."

"Huh." I paused, pondering how to phrase my next question. "How do they, do you, um—" I frowned at my ineloquence "—feed?"

He smiled, and a snick sounded from inside his mouth. Two fangs appeared where his canines would be.

Leaning closer, I reached a hand toward his lips with a curious expression. He opened wider in response. Using my thumb, I rubbed the tip of one sharp point. Just the slight brush pricked my skin, causing me to jerk my hand back and cradle it in my lap. Inspecting my digit, I watched as blood slowly welled up from the half-inch surgical cut. Unhappy with my own clumsiness, I stuck my thumb into my mouth.

His eyes were hooded as his tongue slipped out to lick the offending fang. Closing his eyes, he seemed to relish the taste. After a beat, his lids opened and need reflected in their dark depths.

I popped my finger out of my mouth and looked at it. The blood was beginning to bead. It rolled down toward the webbing of my palm.

He tracked the movement.

Even more curious now, I held out my hand.

Gently, he gently gripped my wrist and brought my hand toward his mouth. A moment passed as he waited to see if I'd change my mind.

I nodded once and focused on his lips. His tongue darted out, catching the dribble before it could escape my upturned palm. The sensation sent tingles through my stomach as he trailed the crimson line back to the source with the flat of his tongue. He paused to see if I would deny him. When I didn't, he took my thumb into his mouth and sucked.

Closing my eyes, I explored the feeling. Heat pooled in between my thighs, and my nipples hardened. Sliding his hand to my inner elbow, he left me to hold my thumb inside his mouth. He swallowed with a groan of ecstasy. The vibration sent a lightning bolt of fire through my arm straight to my core, and set off a moan of my own.

Reaching out, I stroked the stubble of his jaw with my other hand before shifting higher to run my fingertips through his damp hair. The silky strands felt baby soft against my skin. I traced the shell of his ear and down his neck. He looked so vulnerable; not a single line marred his handsome face. His grip moved to my waist. Softly, he began kneading the muscles under my ribs.

Brazen by his response, I shifted onto my knees and straddled his hips. Goddess, he smelled so good. Crisp like the ocean on a foggy morning with a musky masculine tone underneath. Delicious. Leaning forward, I inhaled with the tip of my nose nuzzled against his throat.

Grasping my rear, he moved me closer. I groaned in response; rock hard, he pressed himself against my heat. My mouth opened against his neck. Swept up in the glorious need alighting my channel, I licked his jugular.

He pulled on my thumb again with a rumbled purr of pleasure.

Something snapped audibly inside me. Salivating, I nipped his lobe. All Mother, he felt so damned good. A red haze clouded my thoughts. I felt different, light-headed. I *needed*, I *wanted...*

Clutching my hips, he rubbed my pelvis against his rigid length.

I lost all control. Gripping his shoulder, I sank my teeth into his neck. Pure bliss exploded on my tongue as I swallowed. So *thirsty*.

He stood, effortlessly holding my weight with one hand and the back of my neck with the other.

We were moving, but I barely noticed.

I *needed…*

Repeatedly, he ground me against him until a wave of bliss rolled through my body. Groaning my completion while still attached to his throat, I pulled again.

MINE.

Without warning, I was weightless.

Mine, my mind stuttered.

A shock of cold and lack of air brought me back to myself as the suction of my lips was broken. Still wrapped around Blaze, water filled my mouth as he kicked us to the surface.

He had thrown us into the pool.

Sputtering, I choked as we broke the surface. Clinging to his shoulders, he pulled us to a submerged ledge. Slapping one hand to his neck, he settled me beside him.

Spitting out pink liquid, I screeched, "What the hell!" Pink? I swallowed hard. I could still taste him.

Mine, my mind whispered.

Embarrassed, I hid behind my now tangled hair. What happened to my braid?

"Soooo," he drew out.

I didn't respond. What the hell was I supposed to say about my behavior?

"Hey," he whispered, tugging on a wet strand. "It's okay."

I let out a hiccuped sob. "What's wrong with me?"

Hooking me with his arm, he murmured, "It's fine. You're okay. It's perfectly normal."

I cried harder.

After a few minutes of release, I composed myself as best as I could. "Are you okay? Did I"—my voice cracked—"hurt you?"

Leaning his chin onto my crown, he shook his head. "No, I'm fine. I do need a small favor though."

Pressing my cheek against his shirt, I addressed the soaked material, "What?"

"Well, I'm still bleeding. Vampire saliva works as an anticoagulant to keep the blood flowing. It can also seal a wound. Any of our kind's saliva would work with a human; however, between two Vampires it's best to use the originator's..."

I froze. "What do I do?"

"You just swipe over it with your tongue. Is that okay?"

I lifted my face from his chest, and my ear popped. Opening and closing my jaw at the pressure change, I finally met his eyes.

Cobalt blue, they sparkled in genuine concern. Concern for me and how I was doing with this new revelation.

I nodded. It was the least I could. *Mine…*

He turned his head to the side while I got to my knees on the narrow ledge. "Ready?"

Trying to ignore the whispers inside my skull, I answered, "Yes."

"It doesn't hurt, so don't worry about that."

I sucked in a deep breath as he released the grip on his neck.

Two small holes, the size of a pencil eraser, marred his perfect skin. Blood welled as I watched. My mouth instantly watered. Gulping loudly, I hesitated. "Um, just lick it?"

"Yes, your saliva will do the rest."

Leaning my face inches from his neck, I placed one hand on his shoulder. Inhaling through my nose, I parsed his savory scent. Moving closer, I opened my mouth. Instinct took over, and I latched on again. Moaning, I took a sip. Exquisite.

Palming my hip, he purred, "Focus, Sora."

Coming back to myself, I swiped my tongue over the punctures and tipped my head back to inspect them. Right before my eyes, they closed like magic, as if they never were. Curious, I checked my thumb. Also completely healed.

Without bothering to check, he whispered, "Perfect."

Blushing, I ducked my head.

Deciding some naughtiness was in order, I clasped my fists together underneath the water and skipped them over the surface.

The mini wave splashed him full in the face.

Laughing at his shocked expression, I kicked off my flats and back stroked across the pool.

In a blur of movement, he grabbed my ankle from below and pulled me under. I came up sputtering in mock outrage. "You'll pay for that!"

"Wanna bet?" He submerged and was at the opposite end near the lagoon before I could utter a response.

Treading water, I giggled. "Show off!"

Within a blink, he pulled my frame into the warm circle of his arms. Smirking, he rumbled, "How shall I pay, my lady?" Spinning us in a fast circle, he let go, and swam for the stairs.

Damn, he looked so good. Little was left to the imagination as he got out. Wet, his clothes molded to every inch of his flawless body. That's it. I was so going to hell.

Sighing, I followed to the edge.

Blaze plucked me from the water, and my teeth immediately started to chatter. Reaching to a rack, he snatched up a fluffy, blue, oversized towel. Wrapping twice around me, he smiled. "Come on, we need to get you warmed up."

Taking my fingers, he led me back to my room.

Good thing the carpet is black, I mused as he closed my door.

Dripping water, he flashed into the bathroom.

Pricking my ears, I heard the squeak of a faucet. Making my way over, I peeked inside.

Blaze sat on the side of the jacuzzi with his large hand under the tap as he tested the temperature. With a satisfied nod, he stood. "Take a bath. Warm up a bit. I have some things I need to address." He paused, and his brows rose hopefully. "Text or call me when you're done?"

Surprised by the earnestness in his gaze, I grinned. "Sure."

His boots squished as he prowled toward me. My heart fluttered inside my chest as he stopped. I closed my eyes, and his fingers tipped my chin up. Softly, he kissed my cheek.

Then he was gone.

Dropping the towel, I quickly peeled out of my soaked clothes. Blech. I was freezing.

Dipping a toe into the water, I sighed. Perfect.

Excited, I hopped in and waited for it to fill enough to test the jets.

Blaze

Leaving Sora alone after she took his blood was more difficult than he thought it would be. Sure, he'd had a few Vampire females in his time, but never had he let a female feed from him.

It was beyond erotic. Her blood in his mouth while she took his vein was almost his undoing. He'd had to stay as level-headed as possible though. He didn't want her to have any regrets after the bloodlust took her, and take her it did, to the point of orgasm. Pleased, he prided himself on her pleasure and subsequent release. The sounds she made were music to his ears as he ground against her.

Shucking his wet clothes, he popped into a smaller shower than he was accustomed.

Replaying every sensation and sound inside his mind, he quickly became enlarged. He stroked himself toward his own release, his mind swirling with her scent. He imagined his mouth buried between her thighs, layered like a delicate flower. Just the thought of how she would taste undid him.

Quickly washing up, he stood under the spray. The thought of her nude form on the other side of the wall made his member bob in approval.

With a heavy sigh, he stepped out and toweled off aggressively. He needed her, wanted her, like he'd never wanted anything in all the 997 years of his second life... The taste of her blood caused his fangs to snick down. He ached to mark her as his and smother her in his scent.

Talking down his raging hormones, he dressed. Picking up his Android, he texted Jackson.

'I'm ready for your report in the suite beside my normal accommodations.'

The phone pinged.

'On my way.'

He paced while he waited. Even though she was right next door, he was restless and agitated. The need to mark her was slowly driving him insane.

A knock sounded at the door. Finally, he thought, and barked a quick, "Enter!"

Jackson strolled in with his chin tucked and his eyes on the floor.

Noting his submissive behavior, Blaze stopped and tried to temper his tone. "Report," he started, tacking on, "please."

Rolling his shoulders back to their normal position, Jackson met his eyes. "Three Shifters tested the ward last night: Bear, Dingo, and Wolf. I believe the Wolf was Mel. Mason reported a large brown Wolf with a bald left foreleg."

Blaze began pacing again.

Taking a breath, Jackson continued, "The same Wolf has been scented once since sundown." He braced himself, seeming to expect a blow.

Blaze tried to pull his power back in. He was probably smothering his own brother with his aggression. "Apologies, Jackson, I'm a bit out of my depth with Sora. Keeping a level head is harder than I'd previously imagined."

Jackson relaxed and snorted. "Trouble in paradise already?"

Blaze chuckled. "Not quite. I just don't want to do anything she might come to regret. She's almost a Fledgling in our world." Staring at the ceiling, he sighed. "It's becoming increasingly difficult to control my instincts. She is here"—he placed his large hand on the wall—"but she is not here." He tapped his chest.

Jackson nodded. "The mating instinct is driving you mad, yes?"

Blaze groaned, "God, yes. I can still scent her on my skin, feel her in my blood." He rubbed his sternum for emphasis.

Sitting on the plush wingback accompanying every room in the house, he tipped his head in thought. "That seems faster than normal, right? I mean, your reaction at the pool was similar to a new pairing. You didn't mark her yet, did you?"

Logically, he knew his brother seated himself so he wouldn't appear as a threat. However, instinct took over and he still growled a warning, *Mine!* Clearing his throat, he bit out, "Not yet." Baring his teeth, he loomed over Jackson threateningly.

Dropping his eyes once more to the floor, Jackson pleaded, "Focus please, Blaze. I am not your enemy. We very well may have a war coming with the Shifters."

Blaze prowled another circuit around the room. After a few moments, he replied, "I'm trying, Jackson. My control is very limited. Please keep all the males in the west wing." Arriving at the bed, he sat heavily. "I don't want to hurt anyone regardless of the outcome with Sora. If you could send the two Mated females out, it would be better. Perhaps she could make a friend or two to help her through the transition." Lying back on the mattress, he locked his hands behind his head. "I am truly sorry. Hopefully this will be resolved soon. Can I count on you to deal with whatever comes from the Shifters?"

Jackson met his gaze. "Always, Brother. Always. I am happy for you." His voice took on a dreamy tone. "Maybe one day, I'll know how it feels."

Blaze sat up and padded over on silent feet. Dropping to his knees before his brother, he knelt like a giant child. Resolute, he swore, "You will. We will not stop searching, I swear it." Jackson was a millennium this year. Blaze refused to lose him to the madness that took hold after walking the Earth for so long without a Mate.

With a far-off smile, Jackson slapped Blaze on the shoulder. "Hope, Brother, that's all we have in this world."

Blaze knelt with his brother's words echoing in his ears long after he departed.

Chapter 7

Sora

A loud knock startled me. Crap, I'd nodded off in the tub. Lifting a pruned hand, I glanced toward the closed entry. "Yes?"

The handle turned. Wavy blond hair preceded Blaze's face as he looked toward the bed. "Sora?"

Cold water sloshed over the edge of the tub. "Just a minute!" Kneeling, I held my breasts with one arm while extending the other to shut the bathroom door. Flipping the drain with the ball of my foot, I snatched a grey towel. Haphazardly wrapping it around my torso, I slipped my way across the travertine floor and peeked out. "Yes?"

He gawked. "Hey. Um, I didn't hear from you. I was a little worried."

Rubbing the sleep from my eyes, I yawned. "Sorry, I dozed off in the tub. Give me a sec."

"Sure."

Shit! Throwing my hands up, I tugged on my wet hair. The man I'd practically taken advantage of was here. In. My. Room. Er, his room. "Dammit," I muttered, tossing a hot-pink AC/DC shirt, leggings, and thong from my bag. Grabbing my slightly damp black bra, I dressed. Finger-combing my hair, I opened the door. "Hey, um, what's up?"

Sitting on the wingback chair, he sighed.

Noting his distress, I zipped to his side. Reaching out, I took his large hand in mine. "What's wrong?"

Smiling softly at my worried expression, he rumbled, "You're embracing your Vampiric side, and, well, to be honest, I'm having difficulty controlling mine as a result."

My brows furrowed. "How so?"

"Can we start where we left off earlier? There's still much you need to learn. We haven't even practiced your magic today."

I pulled my fingers from his grasp, and apprehension fluttered through my stomach. Settling on the mattress, I nodded. "Okay. Fire away."

Resting his head on the chair back, he once again adopted his lecturing tone. "We've covered a portion of my Menagerie, but not all. I took in multiple members of the Felidae family when Mel turned them out. Twenty-seven, actually." At my queer look, he specified, "Feline Shifters. They address much of our security and work closely with our Protectors. Now that brings me to the Protectors. They are comprised entirely of my Menagerie. Humans who have increased physical attributes, strength, speed, agility, and longer life spans. They regularly drink small donated amounts of our blood to gain and keep those attributes. The Protectors and Feline Shifters work and train together with a military-like efficiency; they even have their own barracks and training grounds."

"What kind of Cats?" I asked, trying to digest all the information.

"Puma, Cheetah, Lynx, Tiger, Leopard, Lion; pretty much all the big cats."

I gestured for him to continue. "I didn't know so many breeds existed as Shifters."

"We also have a Mage. However, she is abroad at the moment."

"That sucks."

He chuckled. "Yes, it does." Sobering, he tipped his head. "That brings me back to you. Dhampirs are only known as myth to our kind, rumored to possess all our strengths, and none of our weaknesses. Add in your Mage heritage, as well as the dose of venom you received—" he inhaled sharply "—I don't really know the extent of your powers. For instance, do you know why I threw us into the pool?"

Cheeks heating, I muttered, "No."

Placing an ankle on the opposite knee, he stared at the ceiling. "It refers to the bloodlust we discussed earlier. The first feed is always the hardest. You couldn't have truly hurt me, but I didn't want to traumatize you either. The pool was a simple solution." Meeting my gaze, want and need reflected inside his dark depths. "I want you to embrace the life you have now, without any regrets. The bloodlust is strong, as I said before, but you're already bouncing back." His lips curled. "It's astonishing, really."

Lightly, I laughed. "Um, thanks?" What was I supposed to say to that? "Wait, I have a question. Where are the female Vampires? I've only seen guys so far."

"That is our final subject. We have only two. Female Vampires are incredibly rare. Most women don't survive being turned, and, no, we don't know why. They are highly sought after and coveted by the opposing sex. To find your Mate…" he rubbed his face "…is almost impossible. Most go mad as they age past a millennium, which is what I believe happened in Seattle."

"Goddess, that sucks too." I couldn't imagine being alone for that long. "One final question, how old are you?"

Blaze stood as I shifted to the edge of the bed in anticipation.

Pacing, he met my eyes from across the room. "I'm in the nine hundred and ninety-seventh year of my second life. Jackson is in his nine hundred and ninety-ninth."

The words echoed inside my mind: 997? 999? Goddess, that was an eternity. After a few moments, I asked the one thing I really wanted to know: "So, you've never met your Mate?"

He evaded, "I have never taken a Mate."

A relieved breath whispered through my clenched teeth.

Mine…

He turned toward the door. "This must be a lot to take in. Would you like to be alone?"

"No!" My abrupt shout startled us both. Every emotion I had rebelled at the thought of being alone. "Um, could you take me to meet them, the females?"

His smile lit. "Yes." Pulling out his shiny phone, he shot off a text. "I've asked them to meet us in the rec room." A second later, his phone pinged. "Let's go."

Before I knew it, we'd arrived. I *was* getting faster.

Blaze went behind the bar and grabbed a bottle of whiskey. Tilting the label toward me, he asked, "Drink?"

Nervously, I answered, "Sure."

He grabbed two glasses and poured while I waited awkwardly. What if they didn't like me? I was already some weird unicorn hybrid. Sighing, I settled on a spinning leather barstool. Funny, I sat on a similar one the night we technically met. Goddess, I was shitfaced that night. Had my tolerance changed? "So"—I nodded toward the cups—"can I still get drunk?"

"Of course, you are still at least half human. It would take me closer to two or three fifths, maybe half that for you. The buzz doesn't last long, but take it slow"—he winked—"just in case."

Giggling like an idiot, I downed the entire glass. Damn, that was good.

Shaking his head, he turned it into a nod as his gaze brightened over my shoulder. "Sora. Meet Allie and Sasha."

Rotating in my chair, I got my first look at the females of my other half.

Beautiful.

One had eyes the color of a lagoon, a pert nose, Irish skin, and full pink lips. Red hair tumbled around her shoulders in a riot of waves. Her green corset revealed cleavage I could only dream of, and trimmed her waist into a perfect hourglass figure. The swell of her hips fit nicely in her cropped jean shorts. She had the nicest legs I had ever seen, and apparently preferred to be barefoot.

The other was just as beautiful. Her mocha skin was absolutely flawless. High cheekbones and sky-blue eyes made her look more like an Amazonian warrior. The mostly shaved, curly black hair atop her head just enhanced her full lips. She was dressed similar to Red, but her corset was black with blue trim. She towered over her polar opposite by at least six inches, and, also sans shoes, her toes were painted silver.

I blushed. "Hello."

Red wiggled her fingers in greeting. "Allie." She gestured to her left. "Sasha."

I tipped my empty glass. "Sora."

Allie approached first with silent footsteps. "What ya pouring, *Master* Blaze?"

He smirked. "The usual, whiskey."

Sasha flashed behind the bar. "That shit is disgusting. Vodka is the only way to go." She grabbed a bottle of Grey Goose from the shelf, and two shot glasses.

Blaze rolled his eyes and shook his head.

Grinning at their banter, I felt more at ease.

Allie made a shooing motion. "All right, Blaze. Pour our girl another, then off with you. We have girl things to discuss and don't need you stinking up the place with all your—" she paused, waving her hand at his massive frame "—masculinity."

Chuckling, Blaze met my eyes with a curious expression.

I nodded. This was kind of fun.

"All right, ladies, I'll leave you to it. Sora, if you need me"—he tapped his cell—"just text, okay?"

Touching my shoulder where I'd put my brick of a phone underneath my bra strap, I patted it. "Will do."

"Blaze!" Sasha shouted in mock outrage. "She's been here for a couple days, and you haven't gotten her a decent phone?" Snickering, she snapper her long fingers. "Better get to it."

He saluted and was gone before I could reply.

"It's not so bad," I said, placing my phone on the bar with a dull thud.

We all laughed at the sound.

"Okay, okay. It is."

Sasha topped off their glasses and came around to sit on the stool beside me. "When I first got here and met him, that was the first thing he did for me. Kind of sweet and insulting at the same time." Fondly, she smirked in remembrance.

Allie sighed. "Me too. He's a good guy though."

I nodded. "He has his moments. Although the mood swings drive me a little crazy."

They both exchanged a knowing look. After a nod from Sasha, Allie became serious. "What has he told you so far?"

I shrugged. "A lot. It's kind of hard to digest."

She looked at me imploringly. "Do you have any questions?"

"Yes, quite a few actually." I sipped my whiskey while bouncing my gaze between them. "Is he really that old?"

Sasha's expression saddened. "Yes. He needs to find a Mate soon. There's just too few of us."

Somberly, Allie continued, "That brings me to my next bit of business." Her lips lifted. "He has it bad for you."

My cheeks reddened.

"Hell yes he does." Sasha pinched my cheek with a smile. "What's not to like? Gorgeous eyes"—she waved a hand at my chest—"rocking body, and hair to die for." Tugging on my braid, she pointed to the wallpaper. "I'm sure you've realized by now that silver is his favorite color."

I rolled my eyes. There *was* a lot of silver and grey everywhere in the house.

"I don't know, guys. I only just met him. I don't even know how *I* feel about everything."

Allie tipped her head in thought. "We didn't know at first either. It started for Von and I with an instant attraction."

Choking on my drink, I coughed, "The Tracker Von?"

She nodded. "Yup, the big dope is my Mate." Fondly, she continued in a dreamy voice, "I love him a lot though. Plus, with the instinct, he was really hard to resist."

"Instinct?" I queried.

Sasha lifted her arms and curled the fingers of both hands to her chest. "It's like your whole body goes crazy with this need."

"*Mine,*" they answered in unison.

I froze. *Mine,* the voice whispered again.

At my stillness, they both bobbed their heads.

Allie grinned. "Yup, that's the one."

In a small voice, I asked, "Does it go away?"

Sasha patted my shoulder. "Not that I've ever seen or heard about."

Thumping my head on the bar, I spoke to the polished oak surface, "What if he doesn't feel the same?"

Allie rubbed circles on the small of my back. "He does. We could feel the roll of his power before we even entered the room. Plus, he ordered all of the males to stay in the west wing until you're settled. We both instantly knew something was going down. The males of our kind get a little… overprotective." Pausing, she lowered her voice. "He doesn't want to have any issues."

Nose pressed firmly against the wood, I murmured, "Issues?"

"Yeah…" Sasha sighed "…fights break out when another male even looks at his Mate if they aren't properly paired."

"Paired," I parroted.

"Joined. When two Mates come together mutually, they, you know, bow chicka bow wow." Allie laughed at her own joke.

Sasha shushed her and stood. "Behave, Allie. This is a lot to take in for her." I followed the sound of her steps with my ears, and she continued, "There's some chemical in their seed. It permanently marks the couple with each other's scent during completion."

I sat up. "So, if we had sex it'd happen?"

She shook her head. "No. It's a multi-leveled thing. There's a blood exchange, and the physical completion of sex. During her orgasm, she triggers his. Only then can it happen."

Allie shoulder-bumped me with a lifted red brow. "So… I assume those are your silver flats I fished out of the pool earlier?"

I gawked for a moment, then laughed, loud and hard. As I snorted, the girls joined in too. Tears rolled down my face. Goddess, this felt nice.

The mood lightened considerably after that. We played a couple games of pool and continued to drink. It was fun. I hadn't had true girlfriends in ages.

Around four in the morning, we decided to call it quits.

Padding back to my room, I texted Blaze.

'Hi ;)'

He replied almost instantly, 'Hey. Have fun?'

'It was pretty awesome.' I hesitated after hitting send. Quickly, I keyed in another response, 'Want to come over?'

'Sure.'

As I climbed the last couple stairs, there he was, waiting at my door. He looked even better to my buzzed mind, if that was possible. Bare, his large feet peeked out from under his grey pajama bottoms. Black, his skintight tee made my mouth water.

Maybe this wasn't such a good idea. Drunk texting is dangerous. Dangerous, I giggled.

His brow furrowed in amusement. "Something funny, Sora?"

I hiccuped. "No, just happy." Beaming a huge smile, I opened the door.

Smirking, he braced one thick arm over my head and held it. "After you."

Chuckling, I moved inside. "So chivalrous."

Janelle Peel

Chapter 8

Blaze

Following the swing of her hips inside, he closed the door. "It went well I take it?"

She swayed at the foot of the bed. Reaching out a hand to the chair to steady herself, she smiled. "Yup." Hiccuping, she twirled around in a circle before falling onto the bed in a fit of laughter. "It was so fun."

He chuckled at her inebriated state. "Just how much did you drink?"

Ignoring his question, she patted the bed. "Come sit with me."

He paced over, and his toes sank into the carpet as he sat. Evidently, that wasn't what she meant. Reaching up, she tugged on his shoulder and pulled him down beside her.

Turning his head toward her, he asked, "Is that vodka on your breath?"

Smiling at the ceiling, she drew out, "Maaaaybe."

That explained the inebriation. Mixing liquor was never a good thing. Hopefully she wouldn't have a hangover tomorrow.

Rolling to her side, she faced him. Pale blue, her half-lidded irises sparkled with inner flecks of light. Like liquid silver, the tips of her unbound tresses fanned out on the bed and tickled his face. Lifting a hand, she traced the stubble of his jaw.

His breath caught.

Quirking her lips, she pinched his cheek. "Hi, handsome."

"Hi back," he rumbled.

She ran her fingers through the short lengths of his hair, her face scrunched in thought. "Blaze."

Reaching over, he smoothed the v of her brow with his thumb. "Yes, Love?"

Her brows dipped as she stared at him. No, through him. Like she could see into the depths of his mind and pluck the answers she sought.

Her hand stilled. "Are you… my Mate?"

The vulnerable tone of her quiet words sent an ache through his chest. He could only hope his answer wouldn't frighten her. Touching her cheek, he whispered, "Yes."

Her eyes widened at his admission.

"It doesn't change anything," he rushed, "unless you want it to."

Rolling onto her back, she trailed her palm across his chest and stared at the ceiling. Her voice softened. "Will you stay with me, to sleep I mean?"

She tipped her chin toward him, and he gazed like a man lost at sea into her swirling depths. "I would do anything for you."

Satisfied with his answer, her lips curled. Lifting her hips, she rolled down her black cotton leggings. Sitting up, she slowly pulled her shirt over her head. Nodding toward the light, she crawled to the head of the bed, flashing him with her perfect heart-shaped rear outlined in a black thong.

Stunned, he watched the rise and fall of her pert breasts the matching bra did little to cover. Leaning forward, she pulled the blanket up to her waist.

A deep purr of appreciation began at the back of his throat. He peeled his tee over his head.

Her gaze pulsed as she tracked his movement.

With a smirk, he flashed over and cut the lights before she could see the evidence of his arousal.

Making his way back to the bed at a human pace, he internally debated, above or below the covers? Deciding to leave the choice to her, he climbed onto the king-size bed and lay back against the soft pillows.

A rough tug answered the question for him as she attempted to pull the blanket out from under him. Tucking his legs, he lifted the duvet and settled back once more.

The sound of fabric rustled as she moved closer. Grabbing his hand, she pulled him onto his side and shifted her body into the shelter of his. Reaching back, she wrangled her hair and twisted it into a loose knot above her head. Gripping his hand, she shifted his arm under her breasts before pressing the curve of her spine against his naked chest.

He could hear her heart pound for a few moments at their closeness. As he was still, it slowed and her breaths evened out.

Snuggling closer, he tried to keep his rigid member from pressing against her rear.

With a soft sigh, she shifted her hips back against him and eliminated his worry.

He stilled. The only separation between their skin was his sweats.

She chuckled softly. "It's fine, Blaze. Rest with me."

Figuring she knew best, he acquiesced and pulled her smaller form closer to his.

Mine…

Sora

I woke to a deep purring sound in my right ear.

Somehow, I ended up sprawled on Blaze's chest with our legs intertwined beneath the covers. Gently, I untucked my leg from his and shifted my hips to get up.

Immediately, his grip tightened around my shoulders as the purring stopped.

"Hey, um, I have to pee," I whispered.

Releasing me, he rumbled a laugh.

Thank the Goddess! My bladder ached. Popping up, I rushed to the bathroom and closed the door.

Finishing up my business, I decided to brush the stank of stale alcohol from my breath.

Padding back into the room, I went to the nightstand for my phone, only it wasn't there. Instead, my fingers closed around a lightweight box. Feeling my way around for the unlock button, it flared to life in the darkened room as my eyes squinted.

Cool, a Galaxy S8. The time read 4:00 p.m.

Blaze sat up. "Do you like it?"

I smiled. "It's awesome." Setting it face down on the table, I crawled back into bed.

Burrowing beneath the covers, I pushed him back against the pillows. Laying my head upon his chest, I wrapped my knee around his firm thigh and tucked my cold toes under his calf. "Hi," I whispered with my minty breath.

"Hey," he growled in a deep baritone.

The playfulness drained from my voice. "What did Jackson want yesterday?"

"He was updating me on security." Sighing, he added, "It seems the Shifter Pack isn't willing to let you go. They know you're here and have been sniffing around the perimeter. They're testing our ward. Mel has been spotted three times along with a Bear and Dingo."

In a small voice, I asked, "What do you think they want with me?"

He tightened his arms around me and answered in a tone that brooked no argument, "It doesn't matter; they can't have you."

I patted his chest soothingly. "I don't want to be a burden."

He tensed. "Never."

"I suppose we should get up and practice magic then?"

"We should, yes, but I am finding it extremely difficult to get out of this bed."

131

I wanted to see his face. Touching my sternum where the well of power resided in my center, I envisioned a ball of light. Lifting my hand, I pushed my will and lit the tips of my fingers. Slowly an orb grew. It flickered inside my upturned palm. When it was the size of a softball, I willed it to hover near the ceiling while holding the tether tightly. The sphere slowly rose until it hovered seven feet above us like a mini sun. Glowing brilliant white, blue flame danced across its surface. Letting out the breath I was holding, I looked up at him.

His face was one of awe… while tinted blue like a Smurf.

I snorted a giggle.

"What's so funny?"

Snickering, I mumbled, "You look like a Smurf."

Shifting onto his elbow, he inspected my face with a lifted brow. "As do you." Tipping his head back to the ceiling, he rumbled, "I wonder, can you make it change colors?"

I focused my will once more, and the ball slowly turned white, then orange and red. I added the blue back to the edges.

"It looks like a campfire. So beautiful…" Only he wasn't looking at the ball.

Blushing, I lay back and watched the flames twirl. They spun, bounced, and flattened. Feeling confident in my ability to forge any shape, I turned it into the bud of a rose. I imagined the perfect red of a bloom as it slowly opened, and each petal glowed with flame. The effect was gorgeous. I added a yellow, pink, and white to my magical bouquet.

With a cracking yawn, I released the tether. The flowers snapped in a shower of white sparkling dust and fell toward us like small stars.

A note of worry entered his deep bass. "Are you all right?"

Around another yawn, I answered, "Fine, just a little tired."

Softly, he chided, "Well you didn't eat yesterday…"

Ugh, really? I quipped, "Well, neither did you."

He chuckled. "Touché. I haven't been able to feed since taking your blood. Even the thought is revolting."

The wheels in my head began turning. I was incredibly thirsty… and his blood was delicious. "Are you hungry then? Just how often do you have to feed?"

He sighed. "Every three or four days, usually."

I pressed, "So you haven't eaten since last week, after the bar?" Mentally I tacked on, "when you attacked me."

"Other than yesterday in the courtyard, no."

Moving my hand slowly, I placed it on his toned pec. Unsure, I asked, "Um, do you need to feed?"

His voice dropped an octave. "Are you offering?"

I debated. Could I do this? It seemed so surreal. On one hand, I wanted him to, and on the other, I really wanted to taste him again. The thought still kind of grossed me out though.

After a moment, I inquired, "How does it work? I mean, will what happened yesterday happen?" Heat pooled low in my belly at the thought.

Lifting a hand, he palmed my cheek. "We can do anything you want. I won't ask you for more than you are willing to give."

My heart warmed. Curious, I lifted a brow. "Can you see me?"

"Yes, we have exceptional night vision. I expect you to as well, eventually."

I was pretty sure he meant with more feedings. "Where, um, do you normally feed from?"

Emotionless, he stated, "The wrist or neck… the inner thigh is also used."

Goddess, the thought of Blaze between my thighs lit my blood on fire. *Mine...*

Trying to corral my wayward thoughts, I lifted my hand and offered my wrist.

Blaze

As she tilted her wrist toward his face, he couldn't quite believe what she was doing. This had to be incredibly difficult for her, but he would not refuse her. He hoped to get her to feed as well.

Gently, he curled his fingers around the back of her small hand and placed his thumb inside her palm.

After a pause, she guided her vein to his mouth. Dipping his head, he savored the heady fragrance of her skin.

A shiver trembled her shoulders in response.

His teeth dropped down with a snick.

She stilled. "Will it hurt?"

Pressing a kiss to her offering, he rumbled, "No, Love, just a pinch. I promise."

With a soft sigh, she nodded.

Needing no further encouragement, he penetrated her flesh with his canines.

She sucked in a sharp breath.

He froze. After a moment, he retracted his fangs and suctioned his lips over the wound. As he pulled, a tiny moan escaped her.

Shifting them both to sit and face one another, he lifted his arm to her mouth.

She licked her lips. Faster than he could track, she gripped his forearm. Inhaling in short bursts, her fangs dropped.

As he drew her blood once more, she pierced his vein. She sighed in contentment, and her fangs snapped up and she swallowed.

He stifled a growl, and his member throbbed at the sight. Watching her drink from him, making her tiny moans of approval, nearly undid him. Taking a few slow sips, he waited until she'd had her fill. He sealed the punctures with his tongue, his mind rolling with her decadence.

Releasing her wrist, he leaned forward and stroked her cheek. "Enough, Love."

Her grip tightened in response. Opening her swirling eyes, he was struck dumb by her beauty.

Taking her hand, he placed it over his heart and began to purr. Slowly, she lifted her mouth and lathered the wound. Crawling atop him, she bent her legs to straddle his hips and pressed the warm juncture of her thighs against him.

Groaning at her heat, he struggled to control himself.

Softly, she whispered, "Was that okay?"

Beating back his need, he whispered, "Yes, it seems you've already mastered the bloodlust. Remarkable."

"You taste so good."

"As do you, Love."

The tone of her phone startled them both. Lifting herself, she braced a hand on his chest and rocked her hips against him. Grumbling in frustration, she crawled across the bed.

He felt bereft for a moment. He wanted her. *Mine…*

With a shake of his head, he tried to clear his thoughts. This had to be on her terms. Only when she was ready would he make her his.

Grabbing her new cell, she chuckled, "When did you have time to do all this? My contacts are already in here."

He smiled at her praise. "My Menagerie is rather adept with electronics. They just needed your phone number." Standing, he turned away to tuck his engorged length beneath the band of his pants.

She gasped. "Blaze!"

He was at her side before she finished her shout. Listening intently for the source of her distress, he growled, "What is it?"

"My friend Vi-Viv texted me," she stammered. "She owns a frozen treats place by the beach. Someone broke in. They trashed her shop and home… she… was bitten by a Wolf."

Shifter bites spread lycanthropy. Agitation shocked through him. "Is she okay?"

"She's at the hospital. Oh Goddess, this is my fault. We have to go, now. Can we go?" The pleading in her voice made his chest ache.

"Of course. It's probably a trap though. I need to check in with Jackson. Get ready, quickly." He snapped his shirt from the floor. "We won't have much time."

"Time?" she questioned.

"If the bite goes untreated, she could turn."

One moment she was on the bed, the next she was in front of him with his face in a vice-like grip. Breathing heavily, she whispered, "What do we do?"

The fear in her voice made all his protective instincts scream. He growled, "We get her and offer her a choice. If we're quick enough, we may be able to turn her into a Vampire. Our Mage isn't here, but we can still try."

She gulped. "Okay, okay. I'll tell her we're coming." Dropping her hands, she ran to the bathroom.

"I'll be next door. Come when you're finished."

Flashing to his room, he quickly dressed in fatigues, shitkickers, and a black tee. Grabbing his leather jacket off the back of the chair, he dialed Jackson.

The call barely connected when he roared, "My room, NOW!"

Four seconds later, Jackson entered. His eyes panned the room for any threats. Finding none, he addressed Blaze. "What's happened?"

"Sora's friend has been attacked. Wolf bite, hospital. Now."

"How big of a team do you want?"

His fangs punched down in response to his rage. "A mix of ten. MOVE!"

"Five minutes," Jackson barked, zipping out of the room and slamming the door.

137

A tapping brought him back to himself.

"Blaze," Sora whispered.

He struggled for calm. "Come."

Entering, she hesitated beside the threshold. Her silver locks were braided tightly down her back and lay against a cropped jacket that matched his. Dark denim hugged her hips, and knee-high boots adorned her feet. Tears slowly tracked down her face.

Rushing to her side, he pulled her into his embrace. "Shh, it'll be fine. We *will* get her back, I promise. We have to go though." He knew he couldn't get her to stay, so he didn't bother wasting the words.

Ten minutes later they were speeding through PB in a blacked-out van. The tension was palpable.

He barked, "ETA?"

Jackson answered, "Three minutes, but I suggest we approach on foot. If this is a trap, I want our teams spread out."

Blaze growled, "Affirmative. Everyone pair up. Sora, Jackson, you're with me. I want teams no less than a block apart surrounding the hospital." His tone softened. "Sora, what floor?"

Hands clenching the leather armrests, her increased strength ripped both at the seams. "Third, room 302."

Jackson began issuing orders, "The best point of entry is the roof. It's only four stories, and the building beside it is a six-story hotel." Tipping the iPad Pro for everyone to see, he flipped the image to an aerial view and tapped the screen. "Mason, I want the pairs scattered throughout these points." Turning to Sora, he tucked his chin. "Sora, could you please describe your friend?"

Releasing her death grip, she wiped her palms on her thighs. "Her name is Viv. She's about five foot tall with green eyes and a spiked pink haircut. She's tiny, maybe 110 pounds."

Everyone nodded.

The vehicle slowed as Jackson peered through the windshield. "We're at the drop. Rendezvous back here in fifteen minutes. Clear?"

Ten voices sounded off, "Affirmative."

He continued, "Jake, Von, guard our ride. We don't want to have to run all the way back with an injured person."

In unison, they replied, "Got it, boss."

"Go!"

Sora

At the word from Blaze, we all scrambled out of the van.

Jackson jerked his head to the tall building a street over from ours.

Blaze nodded.

We followed him at Vampire speed to the hotel's back door. Using magic, he manipulated the lock and opened it with a soft click. As we filed in, he closed it quietly and relocked the handle.

Unsure of my role, I fidgeted.

Blaze grabbed my hand and pulled me to the stairwell. Jackson led as we zipped up six flights of concrete steps.

Barely winded, I marveled at our speed.

Looking to Blaze, he counted down from three on his fingers and soundlessly pushed through the roof access.

Empty, we crept to the edge. Both Vampires took small breaths through their noses.

I didn't smell anything other than ozone from the running HVAC unit.

Leaning down to my ear, Blaze whispered, "We will go first. After it's clear, I'll signal you to follow. Watch what I do for the jump." Settling his massive hand on my shoulder, he squeezed once in reassurance. "I know you can do this."

His confidence bolstered my morale. "Got it, easy peasy."

He pressed a chaste kiss to my temple, and his gaze darkened. "That's my girl."

In a blink, Jackson leapt from the building. Sailing over the sidewalk below, he landed two stories down.

Blaze stepped to the ledge. At my nod, he vaulted over.

They landed so quietly, I thought, watching as they zipped around the hospital's rooftop.

A scuff drew my attention. Panning my gaze, I sniffed. The musky scent of an animal filtered on the breeze.

Goddess, I wasn't alone. In full-on panic mode, my thoughts spun. Jump, or fight?

Something slammed into me from behind, knocking me to the roughly tarred surface. Pieces of gravel stuck to my bare palms as I rolled with the motion. Coming to a stop, I looked up.

Mel stared back. A shimmer lit his large frame. Instantly, his clothes shredded to leave a huge brown Wolf standing in his place.

Shit! He must have scaled the wall in human form. My eyes snagged on the small bald spot. It seemed his fur was growing back.

Following my gaze, his hackles rose with a snarl.

Lifting my hands, I got to my feet. "It was an accident, I swear!"

Unimpressed with my answer, the growling increased. His back legs bunched as he readied to pounce.

Fuck that! I turned on my heel to run, but his large teeth latched onto my shoulder. Lightly, his sharp teeth pierced my skin through the leather. Tossing his head, he jerked me back to the ground.

Rumbling a warning, he shifted his maw to the collar of my jacket and began dragging me toward the stairs.

Hell no! My hands lit. Blindly I slapped at his face and connected with his snout.

Grumbling in pain, he dropped my jacket and backed away. Flattening his ears, he let out a quick yip. Another echoed from the stairwell.

There was at least one more headed my way.

Frantically, I stood and eyed the distance for my escape.

Seeing my intent, he prowled forward with a growl. The sound raised every hair on my body.

Throwing out my arms, I tried to remember the flames I used before. Envisioning it, I drew a line of pure white between us. I backed away as black smoke thickened the air. As I neared the ledge, two more Wolves joined Mel.

Turning, I jumped. The freefall dropped my stomach as I fell like a flaming comet to the opposite roof. I hit its surface in an ungainly heap, and my ankle throbbed as I staggered to my feet. Looking up, the Wolves paced in agitation.

Instantly, Blaze flashed to my side. Fangs fully extended, he hissed, "What happened?"

Grabbing his shoulder, I stumbled to the door. "Later. We have to get Viv."

Scooping me into his arms, he zipped us inside. Gently, he propped my battered frame up on the landing. Cocking his head, he appeared to listen. "Jackson has her. They're coming up. We need to find another way out."

Rounding the corner below us, Jackson appeared with a tiny pink tuft of hair sticking out from the crook of his elbow. A huge hospital gown covered half of his chest, and magenta-colored Chucks dangled near his hip.

"We need a new exit," Blaze barked. "The Wolves attacked Sora on the roof."

Jackson's eyes widened. "Were you bitten?"

A loud rumble began as Blaze ground out, "Were you?"

"It's just a scratch. My jacket got the worst of it." My eyes bounced back and forth between them. "What?"

Neither responded.

Jackson turned. "Let's go. There's a skywalk on this floor that leads to a separate wing across the street."

Blaze picked me up. The halls blurred with the motion. Ugh. I didn't feel so well.

Clinging to his jacket with sweaty hands, my lids lowered.

The next thing I knew, we were in the van. Everyone was quiet. Dryly, I attempted to swallow. Working my tongue around, I mumbled against Blaze's shirt, "We did good?"

Worriedly, he whispered, "Yes. We're almost home."

"Did she try her magic?" Jackson's voice sounded.

Struggling against the tide, I tried to pry open my eyes. My entire body ached.

With more difficulty than I'd like, my lids fluttered. Almost there.

Finally, they opened. I was still tucked into the shelter of Blaze's arms. Panning my surroundings, I noted we were in my, no his, maybe our room.

"Not yet," Blaze grouched.

My voice cracked. "Hey. So thirsty."

Jackson stated the obvious, "She needs to feed."

Blaze threw him a glare.

Placatingly, Jackson moved to the door and muttered, "Okay, okay. I'll be outside if you need me."

As he exited, Blaze shifted me to one side and pulled back his sleeve. "Feed, Love."

His tone frightened me. What was wrong? My brows lowered, silent in question.

Heaving a sigh at my stubbornness, he answered, "Wolves have venom too. That's how they can turn others. I don't know how it will affect you since you are still half human. You need to feed and use your magic." Pleadingly, he added, "Please, Love?"

My heart hurt at his tone. Obediently, I opened my mouth and snicked down my fangs. Too weak to lift my head, he brought his wrist to my mouth and pressed against my canines. Retracting them, I drank, deeply. All Mother, he tasted so good. Salty and sweet at the same time.

Satisfied I was doing as he asked, he relaxed.

I closed my eyes and swallowed.

A tap on my nose made me open them again. Anxiously, Blaze loomed over me. Breaking the suction, I lathered the punctures.

"Better?"

I nodded. "A little. Help me sit up?"

Resituating me across his lap, he supported my upper body with one arm. "I need to take off your jacket and open your shirt. It might sting."

I jerked my chin as he tugged one cuff down. Then I gritted my teeth as the other side unpeeled from my injured shoulder. A small whimper escaped as he ripped open the collar of my shirt.

Inspecting the damage, he growled, "Just barely. The venom is setting though. Can you call your flames?"

Reaching for my center, I noticed it seemed dimmer than before. Sweat broke out on my brow as I tried to corral it. The seconds seemed to drag on like hours. Finally, I tugged it free and looked at my hand. It glowed green, not my normal blue. Shaking my hand, I screeched, "What. The. Fuck!"

Grabbing my flailing limb, he snapped, "Sora! Focus."

Gently, I put my hand on the wound. Closing my lids in discomfort, I reached for my well. Slippery, the fire flickered in and out of my grasp. Throwing a tether, I linked it to my wound and bent it to my will. White light glowed, coloring spots in my vision as my magic took over. Faster the flames spun in my mind's eye until they sparkled aqua once more. Thank the Goddess!

No longer feeling pain, I opened my eyes. Dancing of their own accord, my silver tresses floated in a halo around my head.

Blaze's soft smile of relief buoyed my own. Lifting my palm, I peeked.

Perfectly smooth, creamy skin greeted me.

He cleared his throat. "How do you feel?"

I took inventory. "My ankle still hurts and I'm a bit tired. Otherwise, I'm fine."

"Good. Your ankle should heal on its own." He paused. "You need to see Viv."

My thoughts raced. What a crappy friend I was! Releasing my power, I wiggled off Blaze's lap. I braced one arm on the nightstand, and a frantic note entered my voice. "Where is she?"

"I had her placed next door. I knew you'd want her close." Rising, he lifted me with ease.

Pacing the hall, Jackson stopped. "It worked?"

We both nodded.

"Hurry up then! She doesn't have a lot of time."

Exchanging baffled expressions, we entered Viv's room.

Janelle Peel

The huge bed all but swallowed her tiny form. Propped against a mountain of pillows, only the top of her head showed. Wheezing, she labored for every breath from her cracked lips.

Blaze set me down.

My knees bumped against the mattress, and my chest pinched. Her complexion, normally tanned by the sun, held a sickly pallor. Sweat dampened her brow as it plastered her hair in clumps across her forehead.

My heart broke. "Oh, Viv, I'm so sorry."

Softly, Blaze touched my shoulder. "She's not gone, Sora. Heal her."

I jerked a nod. I could do this.

Jackson padded around the other side of the bed and pulled her swollen arm from beneath the covers.

Six punctures, oozing green pus, lined the top of her hand. As he turned her palm over, four more identical marks pierced her flesh. Gently, he settled her limb back on the blanket.

Sitting, I moved my fingers under hers. She didn't respond.

Closing my eyes, I focused again. My well glowed a healthy blue. I envisioned a rope of light unwinding from my center and looping around our joined hands. I pressed my will, and heat filled my palm. White light shone against my closed lids as I prayed to the All Mother to help me save my friend.

Jackson gasped.

Slowly, I opened my eyes.

Crystal clear, her green gaze met mine shining with tears. A small smile lit her face as she took in the glow of my magic. "It's beautiful."

Elated, I beamed, "Thank you."

I released her grip, and the glow faded. The punctures were gone.

Curiously, I asked Blaze, "Is that enough?"

"To offer her a choice, yes." He frowned. "The full Moon is tomorrow. She will have to decide before it rises."

Viv's nose scrunched in confusion.

"Shh," I soothed. "I will explain. You're going to be okay."

Jackson cleared his throat. "I can do it."

Viv ping-ponged between us. Taking in Jackson's wiry frame, she smirked. "You carried me, right?"

He bowed his head. "It was my honor."

She snarked, "And just who the hell are you?"

I giggled. My friend was back.

"J-Jackson," he stammered, thrown by her frankness.

I interrupted, "Viv, this is Blaze, and his brother, Jackson. Think of it kind of like an episode of *Supernatural*. You were bitten by a Wolf Shifter, unfortunately. These two are Vampires." As I hooked a thumb at myself, her eyes rounded. "And I'm some weird Magical Vampire Hybrid."

Her mouth opened and closed for a minute. Finally, she nodded. "Decide what?"

I bit my lip. "Well, you've been bitten, so you're going to turn into a Werewolf. Unless you want to be a

Vampire. Then we can try to do that. You have until tomorrow before the Moon rises to decide."

Blaze rumbled in disapproval, "If you remain a Shifter, the Alpha who bit you can claim you as Pack. You would be his."

Without missing a beat, she queried, "Can I go back to my life with either option?"

Sadly, I shook my head. "You couldn't be with Jason either."

Jackson let out a growl. Instantly, I snapped my gaze to his. "Stop."

Blaze sighed as he took in his brother's frozen form. "Sora, Love, you can't do that. I don't want anyone knowing about this particular talent of yours yet. Please?"

Chagrined, I muttered, "You're right, sorry. I just didn't want him to scare her."

Viv stared at Jackson's still form. Shrugging it off, she mumbled, "We broke up. He was a douche."

I gave her a sympathetic look. Turning, I made eye contact with Jackson. "Forget the last two minutes. As you were."

Jackson unfroze. Confused, he panned the room.

Trying to stay on topic, I continued, "Anyway, you will have to cut all your human ties."

Her brows dipped. "My shop?"

Factually, Jackson answered, "You'd need to sell it. We would help with whatever you need."

"Okay. I know what I want."

I held up a hand. "No, please. This is a lot to digest. Take a couple hours at least. This is a big decision.

Have a shower and rest. I have some clothes you can borrow. Okay?"

She nodded.

Rising, I gestured in a shooing motion. "Okay, boys. Off with you. Blaze, I'm taking her to our room." Immediately, I slapped a hand over my mouth. I'd said *our* room.

Grinning, Blaze moved to the door. "Sounds good." Turning the handle, he called over his shoulder, "Let's get a drink, Jackson."

Jackson looked from Blaze to Viv, shook his head, and followed his brother out.

With a sigh, I helped Viv out of the giant bed.

She chuckled. "Our room, huh?"

I blushed.

"Do they all look so perfect?"

"Yup." Changing the subject, I sang, "You're going to die when you see the shower!"

Chapter 9

Viv

As Sora pulled me to her room next door, I wasn't sure what to think. I mean, I'd seen the shows, read the books, but where did make-believe end and reality begin?

Leading me to her bathroom, she flourished with a bow. "My humble accommodations await."

Giggling at her glibness, my pink Chucks slapped against the travertine floor. Jesus, the jacuzzi was almost double my height and five times my width. I marveled at every jet. Shit, this was amazing. Eagerly, I began toeing off my shoes in preparation for the best bath of my life.

"Nope. That's not for you." She flipped a switch on the wall. "Try this."

My gaze flipped to hers, then the tumbling waterfall, and back again. Incredulous, I asked, "Are you serious?"

She smirked. "Yup. My clothes are in the bag by the door when you're finished. I should have some cropped leggings that'll fit you like pants, and my tees will be tunics on you." Tapping her chin, she grabbed a fluffy, grey towel from a shelf. "You'll have to go commando though." Grinning, she moved over the threshold and tossed it over. "I'm sure no one will mind."

Cheeks heating, I shouted, "You ass!"

Every guy I'd seen looked perfect, but I had bigger things to worry about.

Turning my back to the vanity, I tried to locate the tie of the hospital gown that was practically strangling me. Christ, you'd think they could have given me a kid gown or something. Finding the string, I gave it a quick jerk.

Shit, now it was all knotted. Genius, Viv, really. Facing the mirror, I stared at my reflection. Ugh, I looked like ran over dog shit.

I flipped open the various drawers and cupboards for scissors, but my search yielded no results. Not even nail clippers. Damn.

I padded back out to the room, but Sora had already gone. Fuck, I really didn't want to go wandering around with my ass flapping in the breeze. Peeking my head out into the hallway, I saw an older man in a white polo and shiny shoes.

"Excuse me?" I called.

Turning with a half bow, he answered, "Yes, Miss Viv?"

At my stupefied expression, he strolled closer. Issuing another half bow, he smiled. "Forgive me. I am

Julian, Head of the Household for Master Blaze. I was previously made aware of your arrival. How may I assist you?"

My eyes squinted at his brown ones. "What, like a butler?"

"Something like that."

Sarcastically, I drew out, "Okaaaay. I need something to cut this hideous tent off." I waved a hand behind my head. "The tie is stuck."

"Right away, Miss Viv. I shall return shortly. Is there anything else you require?"

Hope filled my voice. "Got any snacks?"

"Yes," he nodded. "We have a fully stocked kitchen. Did you have anything in mind?"

Hmm, I thought for a moment. "Any kind of meat, please." Holding out my palm, I added, "And call me Viv."

He gazed at my hand for a beat before reaching out and clasping my fingers. "Pleasure to meet you, Mi-," he stuttered, "Viv." Releasing his grip, he seemed baffled by our exchange. Shrugging his shoulders, he inquired, "A drink, perhaps, to accompany your food?"

I tapped my chin. "Good question. A Long Island Iced Tea if you don't mind. It's been a hell of a night."

Bowing again, he murmured, "Straight away." Turning on his heel, he strode back down the hall.

Strange, but I could definitely get used to a butler.

Closing the door, I made my way to Sora's bag and began rummaging around. Crap, she was so tall compared to me. Finally, I located a pair of black leggings and selected a tee at random.

A sharp knock drew my attention.

"Just a sec!" I hollered.

Placing my selections on the counter, I rushed to the entry and tugged it open. "That sure was—"

Standing in the hall with a pair of scissors was Jackson. Why did he look so attractive? I never went for military men, they usually had too much baggage, but I'd be damned if I didn't give him a second look. He still wore black fatigues and combat boots laced up to his calves. The tee highlighted his broad chest, leaving little to the imagination of his figure as it cut a tight v at his hips. The thin black fabric highlighted every strand of thickly corded muscle. Yummy.

Clearing his throat, he interrupted my ogling. I could have stared all day.

"Yes?" I asked, meeting his dark eyes almost twelve inches above my own.

Smirking, he paused. Manipulating the sharp blades with his fingers, he made a snipping sound. "Do you still require assistance?"

Sighing, I stepped back and opened the door wider.

Walking to the bathroom, I gestured at the knot behind my neck with one hand, and held the lower half closed with the other. "They tried to strangle me at the hospital with camping supplies. Can you cut the knot?"

I watched his approach in the mirror. His eyes were glued to my neck with such intensity I shivered. Noticing my discomfort, he shifted his attention lower to the knot in question.

As I focused on the silver-veined marble surrounding the sink, he gently grabbed the gown's tie.

Shifting his grip, the tips of his fingers touched my neck. An entirely different kind of shiver raised goosebumps along my skin.

"Sorry," he mumbled.

Snip.

Moving my palm over my heart to keep the material from sliding down, I smiled. "You're fine, thank you."

No response.

Curious, I peered again at his reflection.

Stock still, he gazed at my bared upper back and shoulders. Hesitantly, his hand reached out then retreated.

I quipped, "Seems like I'm not the only one enjoying the show."

He stepped back, and his face shuttered. "Will that be all?"

"Yup, I'm good here. Julian said he'd bring me some food." When he didn't reply, I raised my voice, "Um, I'd really like to take a shower now. I feel disgusting."

His brows furrowed.

What the hell did he have to be confused about? Okaaay, weird Vampire in my bathroom... Time to go.

I jerked my head to the door. "Thanks for your help. You can see yourself out?"

"Of course." He straightened his shoulders and left.

Strange.

Shaking it off, I dropped the tent and hopped into the glorious running water.

Jackson

Well, that could have gone better. He couldn't believe he just stood there like some perv. She was incredibly distracting though. Those bottle-green eyes, dark lashes, and short pink hair like a rocked-out pixie... Her lithe frame called to him, something that'd never happened before.

He didn't know how long he stood outside the bedroom door before hearing Julian's shoes whispering his approach on the stairs.

Turning, he addressed the Head of the House, "Hey, Julian."

Clearing the final step, Julian shifted his tray and bowed. "Jackson, do you require assistance?"

"No, no. I was just helping Viv with her gown."

Julian quirked a brow. "Perhaps you would like to deliver her food as well?"

Jackson paused. He wanted to see her again but wasn't sure if she'd be happy with him doing so.

"No, thank you."

Sora

As I spun on my barstool in the rec room, I wondered at Jackson's reaction to Viv.

"Another drink?" Blaze questioned.

"Sure."

"There's something you should know. It really doesn't change anything, and I don't want to alarm you." He sipped his drink before continuing, "The dire-fire you used on the roof burned the hotel to the ground." At my horrified expression, he rushed, "Everyone got out. No one was injured. I've already made arrangements to help anyone in need, and have a broker trying to purchase the land for the original price it was listed for. Luck would have it the owners were trying to sell and it was mostly vacant."

I sucked in a breath. How could I have been so reckless? I knew that dire-fire burned everything in its path to ash. I'd let my fear override my reasoning and had ruined countless lives. All Mother, I prayed, please forgive me.

Noting my self-pity, he laid a reassuring hand upon mine. "I've taken care of everything, I promise. There is something else, however."

My brows furrowed. What could be worse than destroying someone else's livelihood, even if by accident?

With a serious face, Blaze answered my unspoken thought. "This won't have gone unnoticed by the Council. They will be looking for a Coven powerful enough to have caused the damage."

Gravity hit and I face planted the bar as my ignorance came full bore.

Wisely, he changed the subject. "So, Jackson and Viv?"

Happy for the reprieve, I shoved all thoughts of the Council to the back burner where they belonged. "His reaction was odd, right? I mean growling and pacing outside her room. It was weird."

Blaze poured another shot as I sat up. Setting the bottle down, he braced his palms on the polished oak. "It's hard to say. He could have been reacting to the stress of the situation." Rubbing his chin, he added, "He isn't usually so emotional though."

Hope colored my response. "Do you think she'll choose to be turned? I don't want to lose my friend."

Sighing, he moved around the bar and settled next to me. "I don't want you to get your hopes up, but who would want to go live with the very people who wrecked her life?"

Smirking at his answer, I hooked a thumb at my chest. "Me. Although, I had previous knowledge of what goes bump in the night. She only has TV shows."

He sipped his whiskey. "True, but she seems to be adjusting very quickly."

I rambled, "She always rolls with the punches. She can stay though, right? If she changes? What is the process for that, anyway?"

Adopting his teacher tone, he answered, "Yes, she can stay. She would have to be bitten and nearly drained of blood. Then she would have to feed from a Vampire. I must warn you though, it is a difficult process, even with the assistance of a Mage. As I said before, we have very few females."

I slapped my hands over my face. We were quite possibly offering her death or the chance to live with the jerks that ruined her life. "What does a Mage do during the process?"

"He or she balances the magic of the Vampire and keeps the blood circulating as the Fledgling is near death. It's like healing, which is why I think you can do it."

Finished with my drink, I stood. "I'm going to talk to her. She should be finished by now."

Blaze rotated toward me. "Do you want me to go with you?"

Pecking his cheek, I smiled. "No, I got it."

Viv

Yum, I thought, popping the last cold cut into my mouth. Julian had arranged for a platter of meats with a perfect Long Island Iced Tea. I was stuffed.

As I got up and wondered where to put my empty platter, the door opened. My heart rate increased for a moment before Sora stepped into the room.

"Hey, feeling better?"

"Tons." I patted my belly for emphasis. "Where do I put this?"

She took the setting from my arms and placed it in the hall on the floor. Crossing the threshold, she paused. "We have a few things we need to talk about."

"Tell me about it—" I wagged my brows "—but first, tell me about Blaze."

Settling beside me, she gathered her thoughts. After a moment, she whispered, "It's complicated."

"Really," I snickered. "Super handsome Vampire meets gorgeous chick… There's a punchline in there somewhere."

She lay back. "Yeah, there is. Blaze is… well, he's my Mate."

I made a pfft noise at her. "Mate. Like you guys go all doggy style, or what?"

We both roared with laughter. Tears streamed down my cheeks as she replied, "No, babe, like soulmates. Female Vampires are really rare. I'm a Dhampir, a living Vampire with all their strengths and none of their weaknesses. I don't have their aversion to the sun, and I don't get weak during the day like they do."

I snarked, "They go all extra crispy KFC or what?"

Trying to suppress her giggles, she snorted. "N-no. I don't know. I'm pretty new to this too. I do have magic though. My parents are some of the most powerful Mages in the world." She waved a hand at my curious look. "Another time. I have magic now; I didn't before last week. Plus, the Dhampir thing." Sighing, she added, "I'm a freaking magical unicorn over here."

We chatted for nearly an hour, when she finally fell silent. Nervously, she fidgeted with the duvet. "What do you think?"

I sighed. "It's a lot to take in." God, I was tired.

Lying back onto the fluffy pillows, I debated my options. Possibly die trying to become a Vampire, or go back to some psycho Shifters. Decisions, decisions. I shrugged. "Vampire."

She cracked a hesitant smile. "Are you sure?"

"Yup"—I held out an open palm—"I have nothing left to go back to. I have you, and I trust you. I could live here in a mansion with a butler—" I gave her a meaningful expression "—a butler, Sora." Flipping open my other hand, I continued, "Or, I could die. Possibly be raped and taken advantage of, or worse, by a bunch of douches."

Sora launched herself at me and squished me in a bone-crushing hug.

"Ease up." I patted her shoulder. "I can't breathe!"

Letting go, she laughed. "Sorry, I'm still getting used to my own strength."

I quipped, "Okay, well don't kill me before I possibly die."

Her face sobered. "I will *NOT* let that happen."

"I know, I know. I just hide behind sarcasm sometimes. Sorry."

Taking my fingers, she squeezed once in reassurance. "I know."

I grinned. "Don't get all mushy on me. Go find tall, dark, and dreamy. I want to get this done."

Nodding, she left.

Well, if I was going to possibly die, I wanted to look my best. Skipping to the bathroom, I decided to ransack Sora's makeup stash.

Sora

I found Blaze on the stool where I'd left him, with the addition of Jackson behind the bar.

Settling in beside Blaze, I tipped my head to Jackson. "Hey."

His fingers tightened on the glass he held. Anxiously, he rumbled, "Has she decided?"

"Yes, she wants to try. I told her all of the risks, but she still wants to do it." I shook my head. "I love her to pieces; I just don't want her to die."

Blaze wrapped his arm around my back. "We will do everything we can."

I dropped my face to the cool oak. "Who does it?"

Squeezing my shoulders, he answered, "Me."

Hot jealousy lit my blood. "No."

Leaning into my ear, he whispered, "It takes a lot of power, Love. The greater a Vampire's power, the better the rate of success. The odds are already stacked against us with her sex."

I heaved a sigh. Rationally, I knew he was making sense, but the thought of him drinking another woman's blood, even if she was my best friend, incensed me. A thud hit the bar as I lifted my head.

In a stony voice, Jackson growled, "I'll do it."

Curiously, I glanced at Blaze. Was this a viable solution?

He rubbed his chin in thought. After a moment, he nodded. "It could definitely work. Your power is closest to my own." Addressing me, he continued, "What do you think? It's your friend's life."

"I think we let her decide."

Jackson
While Blaze and Sora went to get Viv, he prepared himself in the room next door.

The thought of his brother's fangs in Viv's neck enraged him. He would do this, if she'd let him. Breathing deeply, he remade the bed with fresh sheets and tried to calm himself.

The scent of sun-ripened cherries fresh from the orchard with hints of lavender soap preceded her arrival. Decadent.

Her short frame strolled into the room. Cocking a hip, she quirked a brow. "Think you can handle this?"

Christ, she looked good enough to eat. Her bright green eyes regarded him from above a pert nose over bow-shaped lips. The black leggings and oversized grey tunic tee did little to hide the curves of her body.

Battered and pink, her Chucks matched the chaotic disarray of her spiky hair.

As his pause lasted a beat too long, she fisted her hands at her waist.

Spunky little thing, he grinned, gesturing to the bed. "Good to go. Settle in."

Viv toed off her shoes while Blaze and Sora entered. Viv sat and patted the mattress for Sora to join her. Once she had settled, they linked hands.

He glanced at his brother looming by the door in silent question. Blaze jerked a short nod. He could do this.

Crawling onto the bed opposite Sora, Jackson looked into Viv's emerald eyes. "Are you ready?"

Frowning, she faced Sora. "Will it hurt?"

Sora raised her thumb and forefinger. "Just a pinch. You'll become sleepy with the blood loss. Just try to stay conscious, all right?"

Her lids slid closed. "Okay. I'm ready."

Jackson tapped her nose. "Look at me."

She opened her eyes. A glaze overtook her green irises, and a half smile lit her face.

"Thrall?" Sora questioned.

Blaze answered, "It'll make it easier on her."

Nodding, Sora squeezed Viv's fingers.

Shifting closer to her neck, Jackson inhaled her delicate scent. Dropping his fangs, he pierced her creamy skin. Retracting them, he slowly began to draw her blood.

Viv moaned softly as a shiver of ecstasy rolled through her small frame. She tasted sweet, like the finest wines from Italy. So lost was he as the delicate flavors washed down his throat, he snarled when someone touched his shoulder.

"Jackson," Blaze growled. "Stop. Start the exchange."

Coming back to himself, he sealed the punctures with his tongue. Lifting himself onto one elbow, he snicked his fangs once more and pierced his wrist. When the blood began to flow, he placed it over Viv's mouth and murmured, "Drink."

At first, she did nothing. Then slowly, she latched on.

White light lit Sora's fingers as Viv swallowed her first mouthful. The glow traced visible lines beneath Viv's skin as it raced through her veins toward her heart.

Jackson tried to ignore the sight of her swallowing his blood.

Mine… a voice whispered.

Focus!

Their blood began to mingle and a shudder overtook Viv. Grabbing Jackson's arm, she positioned his wrist more firmly against her mouth. Her green eyes sparkled with starlight before slowly changing to the oceanic color of his. She shuddered again. Her body glowed brighter as Sora's magic pushed his blood through her circulatory system.

Blaze rumbled, "That's enough."

Jackson tried to extract his wrist. Growling, Viv clenched his arm tighter. He tried to pry open her fingers, but she thrashed her legs in response.

Sora took a deep breath and gazed into Viv's eyes. "Release him."

Instantly, Viv stilled and let go.

Jackson looked at Sora, then Blaze, and back again. Sealing his wound, he shouted, "What the hell was that?"

Blaze shook his head.

Sora calmly answered, "I can control our kind."

Throwing a glare at Blaze, he bit out, "We will discuss this later." Turning back to Viv's frozen form, he softened his tone in concern. "Is she okay?"

"I don't know," Sora whispered, cutting off her magic. Gently, she palmed Viv's forehead. Looking deeply into her eyes, she murmured, "Sleep until the sun goes down."

Viv obediently closed her lids.

Blaze rumbled beside him, "Let's get some rest. We can discuss all of this tonight." He placed his hand on Jackson's shoulder. "You'll need to rest here with her. Just in case she wakes."

Jackson nodded.

After they left, he lay back next to Viv and held her tiny hand in his much larger one.

Jackson woke to the sound of choking.

Viv!

Reaching out, he sought her frame beside him, only she wasn't there.

In a panic, he flashed to the bathroom.

Leaning over the sink, she coughed up her last human meal.

He rushed to her side and placed his hand on the small of her back. "Hey, shhhh. It's okay."

Lifting her head, her dark eyes shimmered with tears. "S-something's w-wrong with m-me."

Taking her shoulders, he pulled her into his arms and noted her increased height. Soothingly, he whispered, "You're all right. Everything is as it should be."

She growled, "No, I ache." Her voice turned hoarse. "I feel like I'm dying."

Holding her at arm's length, he firmly stated, "No. It's only the transition. You'll be fine."

Her teeth snicked down at his tone. Smirking, she shoved him against the tiled wall. Standing on her tiptoes, she pressed his head to the side and sunk her fangs deep into his throat.

He was so stunned by her sudden movement, he didn't react at first. Her smaller frame felt so good against his.

Then she suckled at his vein. Grabbing her hips, he pushed her back to the vanity. She rumbled a warning at the abrupt movement, but promptly turned it into a moan when he lifted her to the countertop and pressed against her She locked her legs around his hips, and he groaned.

Viv

The press of a hard body against my throbbing core brought me back to myself. Swallowing whatever deliciousness was on my tongue, my mouth made a wet slurp as I leaned back.

Questioningly, I met Jackson's gaze.

Slapping a hand to his neck, he roughly whispered, "Hey."

Confused, I looked around the room. A bathroom to be exact. Repeating silver-lined wallpaper met a grey-flecked travertine floor. The glass-enclosed shower stood off to the side. My ass was on a marble vanity, and the spout from the sink was digging into my back.

"Jackson?" I queried, wondering what the hell was going on.

"Shh," he soothed, rubbing my shoulder. "How much do you remember?"

I snarked, "Evidently not enough. Why the fuck is your dick pressed against my thigh?"

He quickly took a step back and averted his eyes. Face shuttering, he replied in a monotone, "I woke to you coughing in the bathroom. When I came in, you seemed to be choking. I tried to console you. I assume your bloodlust kicked in and you latched onto my neck. I apologize. I could scent your need and I just," he paused and whispered, "responded."

Shamefully, he stared at the floor.

I hopped off the counter just as a quick series of knocks sounded at the bedroom door.

Sora

When I knocked the second time, I became worried. I hadn't seen her since the early hours of the day. What changes would she have gone through?

Blaze was a stoic mass at my back as we waited.

Finally, I heard movement through the thick mahogany. With a click, it opened to reveal a much taller version of my pink-haired friend. Not meeting my gaze, she stepped back and gestured for us to enter.

Blaze hovered in the entry while I made a beeline for the leather wingback. My voice wobbled, "Hey."

Padding to the other side of the room, she blandly mumbled, "Hey."

Awkwardly, I babbled, "What's wrong? Are you okay?"

She took a deep breath, and the air slowly hissed from her clenched teeth. Sarcastically, she replied, "Oh, it's just fine. Right, Jackson?"

Prowling in from the bathroom, he held a hand to his neck. "Yes. Everything seems to be all right." Blood lingered on his collarbone.

I read the situation, and my cheeks reddened. "Did, uh, we interrupt something?"

They replied at the same time.

"Nope."

"Yes."

Viv growled, "No."

I looked to Blaze, who was gazing at Jackson with a raised brow.

Without warning, everything blurred.

One second Viv was on the other side of the room; the next Blaze had her restrained against his chest.

Baring his fangs, Jackson hissed from the bed as he prepared to leap at Blaze.

"Stop!" I cried, scrambling to my feet and lighting the room in azure flames. Jackson froze with a drop of venom poised on the tip of his elongated canine. A crimson line dribbled down his neck and began seeping into the fabric of his shirt.

Desperately, I tried to figure out what happened as Viv stood statuesque inside Blaze's arms.

Turning his head toward me, he rumbled, "It's the bloodlust. She can scent you."

I gasped. Goddess, my friend tried to attack me. "What do we do?"

Releasing Viv, he sighed. "She needs to feed. I'm guessing she attacked Jackson. Order her to seal the wound."

I stammered, "Vi-Viv, lick Jackson's punctures."

With robotic movements, she paced over to his crouched form and licked him from his collar to his ear. Straightening, she awaited further instructions as the small wounds closed.

Standing, I moved to her side. Tipping my head, I whispered into her ear, "You will no longer crave my blood. You will only feed with permission from whoever's vein you're taking. Understood?"

Without emotion, she answered, "Yes."

Blaze touched my shoulder. "Ask her to go back where she was. Tell her to forget the last few minutes. I don't think she would want to remember this."

I didn't want to remember my best friend trying to attack me either. Sighing, I did as he asked, shook out my flames, and released the compulsion.

Jackson's hiss restarted. Abruptly it cut off as he noticed Viv on the other side of the room giving him a curious expression. Retracting his fangs, he threw me a glare and rumbled disapprovingly, "Viv, could you stay in the room for a moment? I need to have a word with my brother and Sora outside."

She nodded. "Uh, sure. Could you get me a drink? I'm so thirsty."

169

Jackson jumped from the mattress, his tone softening. "Of course."

Once in the hall, Jackson lit into me. "How could you do that? No more! Never again, am I fucking clear?"

Blaze growled behind him, "Careful, Brother, Sora was defending herself. You should have been better prepared for her bloodlust in the first place."

Jackson's shoulders slumped. Turning on his heel, he paced across the carpet. "I know, I'm sorry." Rubbing his face, he added, "I just didn't expect it so soon."

I patted his shoulder. "It's okay. She won't feed again from anyone without permission. I don't know how long it will last, so you'll need to stay by her side."

In a lost voice, he asked, "Will she remember?"

I shook my head, then shrugged. "Regardless, go get her a, um, a blood bag. We'll stay here with her until you return."

Nodding, he flashed down the stairs.

Looking to Blaze, I tilted my head toward the door.

It felt a bit like déjà vu as we entered the room again.

Trying to make light of the situation, I smiled. "Hey, are you feeling okay?"

"Yeah, just thirsty."

"Have you noticed your height?"

Glancing down at her leggings, she sucked in a breath at their shortened length. "Whoa!" Lifting her hands, she inspected them too.

I grinned. "Let's go look."

In the mirror, Viv stared at her face for a good five minutes. "What happened to my eyes?"

"All Vampires have eyes the color of the ocean. They change with their moods. Yours are different though. Gorgeous; I love the green flecks."

Her cheeks heated as she leaned closer to check out her complexion.

"I'm sure Jackson's back now if—" I started, but she'd already blurred to the other room.

Chuckling at her enthusiasm, I followed.

Her fangs had already punctured the bag in Jackson's outstretched palm. Adoration marked his expression as she slurped.

"All right, just find me later," I mumbled, giving Jackson the eye to make sure he'd relay the message.

I grabbed Blaze's hand, and we left them to it.

Janelle Peel

Chapter 10

Blaze

As he walked with Sora to the courtyard, he texted his lead Protector: 'Report.'

Mason's response was near instant, 'There's an issue with the ward, sir. Can you send Jackson? I am having trouble contacting him.'

Issues? He already had enough issues. With a sigh, he typed, 'Negative. I'm on my way.'

"Sora, I need to make a side trip to the barracks. Would you like to come?"

"Is everything all right?"

Frustration laced his reply. "No, there is an issue with the ward."

Wiggling her fingers, she nodded. "Sure. Maybe I can help."

Sora

While our feet tapped a rhythmic tone on the rough concrete, I marveled at the construction of the tube. It was just like the movies.

Grinning, I peered at Blaze. "Just how rich are you to have underground tunnels? They must have cost a fortune and taken forever with all the steel reinforcements." I waved at the walls.

The corner of his lip rose. "You'd be surprised, actually. It was a group effort. Vampires are incredibly strong, and with the help of the Shifters and Protectors, what would have taken months, only took a week. The longest part was waiting for the concrete to cure. As to the Clutch's finances, we have done very well on many of our investments over the years."

"I suppose that makes sense." Winking, I added, "Being crazy old like you are."

He looked down with a devilish twinkle in his eye. "Old, huh? Race you."

Before I could blink, he was gone.

"Cheater!" I yelled, picking up my pace.

Blaze was waiting for me at a solid steel door. I tried to shove him, but it was like moving a mountain. "Jerk," I joked.

Chuckling at my expense, he turned the handle and pulled it open with ease.

The small chamber's only furnishing was a lone black bench off to the side. It was made of reinforced steel, and the welded pieces were joined by rivets the size of quarters.

Closing the door behind us with a thud, Blaze shouted, "Mason!"

Seconds later, the heavy tread of boots met my ears from a metal tube leading down from the ceiling.

A large man in fatigues dropped down the last few rungs of the rebar ladder built into the wall. Striking blue eyes met mine over a narrow nose and square jaw. His black hair was styled in a no-nonsense military cut.

I lifted my hand. "Hi."

Blaze rumbled, "Mason, this is my Mate, Sora."

Smiling, Mason tipped his head. "An honor to meet you, Sora. I was with the group who helped rescue your friend."

My cheeks blushed as Blaze growled a warning. Mason snapped to attention and barked a quick, "Yes, sir!"

Blaze clenched his teeth. "Report."

"Sir, this afternoon the ward was weakened. It is still holding, but the Pack has been relentlessly testing it. I fear we don't have long before it breaks."

Pondering the situation, I looked to Blaze's face. His granite-like expression screamed how disturbed he was by Mason's answer. Touching his wrist to calm him, I turned to the Protector. "Can I see the ward?"

Mason's eyes widened as he continued his thousand-yard stare.

Blaze gripped my hand tightly. "Yes. Mason, contact Missy, Von, and Jake. We will go to the perimeter shortly."

"Sir!" Mason snapped his heels and flashed back up the steel tube.

"Who's Missy?" I questioned.

"Our Tiger Shifter. She's fast and resourceful. I don't want to be caught unawares if the ward breaks before we can repair it." He ran his fingers through his blond hair. "Gods, I wish our Mage was here."

Rubbing circles inside his palm, I quipped, "Well, I'm here. We'll make it work."

"I know, we will try. The perimeter is large," he cautioned. "I don't want you overtaxing yourself. You must promise me you will be careful. If you feel faint, you may need to feed in front of everyone."

Eyes wide, I squeaked, "In front of everyone?"

Leaning down, he kissed my cheek. "Yes."

I could do this. This was becoming my home, and I would protect it. I squared my shoulders, and determination colored my voice. "I can do it."

"That's my girl."

After we zipped up the tube, the room opened to the living quarters of the Protectors and Shifters. Multiple bunks lined the stainless walls, and a small kitchenette was tucked away in the corner.

Von and Jake were just as I recalled.

Missy, though, was lovely.

Slightly shorter than my five-foot-nine height, her lithe frame spoke of grace and stealth. Multifaceted caramel and honey highlights, her hair feathered against the line of her chin. Amber eyes assessed me from a sun-kissed face. Tucked into camouflaged fatigues, her black tank outlined the curve of her small breasts.

She snapped to attention as Blaze loomed behind my back. "Sir."

"Missy, this is Sora, my Mate."

Intimidating much? Geez. "Hello, Missy."

Flaring her nostrils, she tipped her head in acknowledgment.

Mason interrupted us, "There has been less activity near the eastern fence line. I suggest we start there."

Blaze took in everyone assembled. "Sora is our main priority. She is the only one who can possibly repair the ward. Understood?"

Four voices answered in unison, "Yes, Sir!"

Mason led, followed by Blaze and me. Von, Jake, and Missy fanned out behind us. Our footsteps were silent as we flashed over a football field's length of wet grass. Just before the ten-foot-tall chain link fence topped with razor wire, we stopped.

Turning, I looked back at the dark shape of the barracks. The Moon was full and would reach its zenith soon. It was so quiet; no owls hooted or coyotes howled in the distance. I shivered: creepy.

Blaze touched my shoulder. His breath caressed my face. "Can you feel it?"

Directing my attention inward, I *could* feel it. The weak hum of magic vibrated at a different frequency than my own. "Yes," I whispered, "it's very weak." Bending my knees, I dropped into a crouch and placed my hand into the soil, searching for the ward. It shimmered in my mind's eye, similar to a silver rubber band about to snap. Funneling power through the tips of my fingers, I tried to keep my flames contained inside my skin. A faint glow lit the earth as my eyes closed to follow the strand. It went on for miles in one large square surrounding the property. I sensed Blaze take a knee behind me, ready to help if need be.

Calling to my well, I shaped the azure energy into a lasso to do as I bade. I threw it around the ward, and my blue shot off for half the silver's length before it began to sputter.

Urgently, I uttered, "Blaze, now."

My teeth snapped down as he pressed his flesh to my mouth. Piercing his vein, I quickly retracted them and pulled. At the first swallow, my flames roared back to life. Red sparks intertwined with my power as it took on a life of its own and completed the circle. As I opened my eyes, the grass lit with a brilliant white line. It pulsed once as my will was done.

Our Clutch was safe.

Ours… mine…

Heady from the rush of energy and Blaze's blood, I slowly lathered the punctures. With a groan, Blaze pulled me to stand and held me in his strong arms. Leaning into him, I looked around at the faces surrounding us.

Mason, Von, and Jake all wore equal expressions of shock.

Missy, however, merely tightened at the corners of her golden eyes.

"What?" I questioned.

Jerking her head, she sneered. "Forgive me. I'm confused. What are you exactly; and if you're his Mate, why can't I scent his mark on you?"

Blaze growled at her challenging tone, "She is my Mate, and that's all you need to know. You're dismissed."

Missy bared her teeth in frustration and stalked off.

Mason came out of his stupor first. "That was incredible!" Visibly excited, he threw his arms wide. "I've never seen such magic! No rituals, spells, nothing." He bowed deeply. "We are truly blessed to have such a member in our Clutch."

Von and Jake also bowed.

"Truly a wonder," Von said, straightening with his gaze glued to the ground.

"Remarkable," Jake cooed, eyes also averted.

Cheeks heating at their praise, I nodded to Blaze. "What is wrong with Missy, and why aren't they looking at me?"

While he took a moment to compose his words, I reflected on all my encounters so far with Vampires of the opposite sex. The only person who'd looked directly at me was Jackson, and Blaze nearly lost his shit as a result. It would challenge him.

Irritated, I spat, "I am not your property."

Blaze cocked a brow. "Shifters are very susceptible to scent, and she's right. My mark is not on you, so she is confused by my calling you Mate. The others"—he nodded to Von and Jake—"are being submissive. Looking at you directly is a challenge not only on my territory, but my status as Master, and my claim to you." He paused. "I told you you're affecting my ability to control myself. I don't want to rush you; I haven't pushed the issue." Lifting a hand, he rubbed his face. "Things have changed though. Jackson was my lieutenant, and with him taking care of Viv, this will only happen more often. The Pack is becoming more insistent in their pursuit of you. Until your decision is made, I can't rule my Clutch properly…"

His voice trailed off as the words rang in my ears. Embarrassed at my naivete, I flashed to the barracks. Pushing my body faster, I flew through the tunnel and into the house. Once I'd reached our room, I slammed the wood panel with a boom.

How could I have been so blind? Blaze rescued me, showed me my magic, and gave me the truth of who and what I was, all the while letting me lead at my own pace.

A light tap sounded on the door.

Throwing myself on the bed, I screamed into a pillow, "I need a minute!"

The bed dipped, then Blaze was there. Gently, he tugged me into his arms.

Frustrated, my tears leaked into the material of his shirt.

"Shh," he soothed. "It's all right."

Biting my lip, I gathered my resolve. "I'm so sick of crying and being afraid."

Kneading the muscles of my back, he rumbled, "I'm sorry. I could have handled that better. I know you're overwhelmed."

Sucking in a breath, I held it for a moment. "No. You have nothing to be sorry for. You tried to tell me, and I just didn't understand."

He stilled.

Decided, in a small, confident voice, I added, "I'm ready. I accept you as my Mate."

His hands clenched around my waist. "Are you sure?"

I didn't answer. Instead, I straddled his hips and braced my palms against his firm chest. Leaning down slowly, I kissed him. As I begged entrance, his hands moved to my silver locks. He ran his fingertips against my scalp, and I shivered.

In a move too quick to follow, he flipped us. He traced my cheek, his gaze meeting mine just before he brushed his lips against my mouth. I opened to him, dancing with his tongue as his stubble scraped against my chin.

Goddess, I had been kissed before, but not like this.

My core ached as my hands roamed the strong lines of his back. Pulling him more firmly against my budded breasts, I tugged on his shirt. I needed to feel his skin against mine.

Shifting to his knees, he chuckled at my impatience. Peeling off his shirt, he tossed it to the floor.

Greedily, I drank in the sight of his perfectly sculpted chest. He looked like a Greek god come alive.

Bending toward me, he brushed his nose along my neck.

Nope, I thought, pushing him back. Gripping the hem of my tunic, I tugged it over my head, baring my pink demi bra.

His eyes roved every inch of my body as he memorized every curve. "Perfection," he whispered, trailing his hand down my flat stomach.

"Move," I commanded, waving for him to stand. I wanted no barriers between us. Slipping from the bed, I flipped open the snaps of my pants, and slowly slid them down my hips.

He watched in stunned silence.

I grinned mischievously. I'd gone commando today. Reaching over, I unhooked the button of his jeans and drew the zipper down. Hmm, he'd gone without as well.

He caught my hand. At my confused expression, he nodded toward the bed.

Swaying my hips enticingly, I crawled back to my original position against the pillows.

Blaze sat and unlaced his boots. They dropped to the floor with audible thumps. Standing again, he pushed the dark fabric down his muscular thighs and sprung his member free.

I gasped at his girth. Goddess, would he fit?

Smirking at my response, he prowled onto the bed. Placing one large hand on my knee, he checked my gaze.

Seeing my need reflected in his own, I slowly opened for him. His hands caressed my inner thighs as he settled himself between my legs. He worshipped my body, kissing a trail from the inside of one hip to my mound. Heat pooled low in my belly as he inhaled to take in my scent. His tongue flicked out and feathered against my slick channel. I moaned at the invasion in delight, savoring every stroke of his ministrations. Inserting a single finger, he *purred*. The intense vibration caused my core to spasm around him.

Rocking my hips, I panted as he thrust in and out of me. Slowly, he drove me toward the abyss. A snick sounded. In a blink, he nicked my swollen nub with one fang. I came apart screaming his name.

Gradually, I came back to myself as my body shuddered with the aftershocks of release.

Blaze worked his way up my body. His deft fingers flipped the clasp of my bra between my breasts.

Tenderly, he worked each one into a hardened peak with his mouth. Sliding the straps down my shoulders, he nipped his way up my neck. Reaching his destination, he kissed me. I could taste the saltiness of my arousal on his tongue. Pulling back, he paused against my entrance. A whimper escaped my lips as he slid over my bundle of nerves. Repeating the motion, he worked me back into a frenzy of need.

I groaned as he pushed into me. Biting his shoulder, I stretched to accommodate his size. As his blood hit my throat, he impaled me to the hilt. I growled in delight. Goddess, he felt so good.

Blaze

As he felt her relax, he slowly drew back and marveled at the tightness of her channel. Entering her fully again, she growled into his ear.

Christ, he didn't know if he would last.

Repeating the motion, she tightened around him with a satisfied groan. Her breasts hardened beneath him, setting off a rumble of his own.

She explored the flexing muscles of his back before settling on the globes of his rear and urging him into a faster pace. Rocking her hips, she met him for each thrust. Just when he thought she was ready, he bit into the vein at her neck. She bit his in return as they both achieved their release.

Her blood mingled with his, marking one another with their scents on a cellular level. As she milked him, another orgasm hit.

Pure bliss and a peace he'd never known overtook his mind. Gently, he closed his punctures.

As she did the same, he rolled her atop him and collapsed, spent from the exertion.

A quiet voice swore… *Mine…*

After their bodies cooled, he decided a bath was in order. Gathering her inside his arms, he padded to the bathroom. He set her on the vanity, and she shivered as her bare cheeks met the cold marble.

Smirking at her reaction, he turned and fiddled with the knobs on the faucet. Dipping a finger beneath the running water, he tested the temperature as the bath began to fill. Satisfied, he lifted her once more and gently placed her in the tub.

A moment later, he joined her.

She mused, "What do we do now?"

He pulled her back to lean against his chest. "Now, we relax. Later I will introduce you to our Clutch. There will be a ball to honor our union." Pausing, he sank them deeper into the warm water. "Then we prepare."

"Ball? Prepare?"

Her anxious response left a sour tang in the back of his throat.

Chuckling, he answered her first question. "We do love our parties, and this is a momentous occasion." In a somber voice, he continued, "Yes, Love. We prepare for war."

Sora

Nervously, I pawed through my meager belongings and tried to think of anything other than the pending war.

184

A ball, he'd said. Who threw balls anymore, anyway? I didn't even own a cocktail dress, let alone a ball gown.

Sighing, I dressed in the only clean outfit I had left. Dark denim cutoffs with a plain cream tee. Plating my silver locks into a tight french braid down my back, I decided I needed to go shopping.

Grabbing my phone off the nightstand, I texted Blaze: 'Hey, I need to go shopping.'

His reply was prompt. 'No, it's too dangerous to leave the mansion.'

Rolling my eyes, I typed back, 'I don't have any clothes, for the ball or in general. I need to go.'

A quick series of knocks sounded on the door. Tossing my cell on the table, I heaved a frustrated sigh and stalked to the door. Tugging it open, I barked, "What?"

Julian's eyes widened at my abrupt welcome. Bowing quickly, he got right to business. "Master Blaze requested I take the liberty to order your clothes in preparation for this occasion."

My face screwed up. "He what?"

Julian motioned with his hand, and Allie stepped into view holding various cardboard boxes.

At my dumbfounded expression, she smiled. "Hey, Sora, where should I put these?"

My mouth snapped closed with an audible click. Stepping back, I gestured toward the bed.

Padding into the room with her bare feet, she smirked at the rumpled duvet. Making a show, she inhaled deeply and lifted a brow.

I blushed. Oh Goddess, could she smell what happened just hours ago?

Julian cleared his throat as my attention swung back to him.

"If anything is not to your satisfaction, or you simply do not want it, please leave it in the hall. I will take care of it."

At my questioning look, he clarified, "The clothes are all in your size." He tipped his head down the hallway where at least twenty more boxes were stacked.

Images of Julian stalking me with a tape measure flashed through my mind. Raising a brow, I queried, "How did you know my size?"

With a slightly patronizing smile, he answered, "I laundered your clothes. Did you not see them in the wardrobe off the bathroom?"

Wardrobe? Flabbergasted, I strode to the room in question. What wardrobe?

Julian's shoes clicked smartly on the travertine as he followed. Bypassing me, he stepped to the other side of the shower and pressed a panel. Whooshing, it slid back into the wall. The lights inside flickered to life.

An entire walk-in closet existed, and I had no clue whatsoever. What the hell?

Julian waved his hand to the left. "This side belongs to you. The other, as I'm sure you can see, belongs to Master Blaze."

Mutely, I nodded as he left with a bow and the tap of his shoes.

Allie joined me. "So… I see you're bonded now." Smirking, she bumped me with her shoulder. "Come on, let's go see your new stuff."

Two hours later, I was exhausted and my room was trashed with discarded boxes. Allie's appetite for fashion was insatiable.

"Okay, mercy!" I cried, throwing myself onto the bed. "No more! I must have tried on like fifty different outfits."

Perching on the wingback, she giggled. "Yeah, but they all looked amazing. Admit it: you enjoyed yourself."

"It was awful," I whined dramatically, fanning my face.

Tutting, she began stacking the torn boxes in the hall. Turning, she lifted a brow expectantly.

"Fine," I grumped, joining her.

Picking up the last piece, she tapped her lips. "I think you should wear the teal number tonight, the backless one with the silver highlights?"

Recalling the gorgeous dress, I nodded. "Which shoes do you think?"

Allie's phone chimed as we stepped into the hall to survey the mess we'd made.

Checking the display, she mumbled, "It's Von. I have to go. Do you need anything else?"

"No." I smiled. "Thanks for everything. It was a lot of fun."

Mischievously, she grinned. "I'll be back with Sasha around six. We'll figure out shoes then… After we do your hair and makeup." In a blur, she flashed down the stairs before I could reply.

Shaking my head, I chuckled at her quick retreat. Seems I was getting a makeover whether I wanted one or not.

My stomach rumbled. Goddess, I was starving after my little runway adventure.

Closing the door, I zipped down the hall toward the kitchen.

Chapter 11

Blaze

After checking in with Jackson for a status on Viv, he found Sora in the kitchen eagerly stuffing fried chicken into her mouth. Smirking, he snatched a paper towel from the counter and handed it to her.

She smiled her thanks and wiped the grease from her cheeks and fingers.

Pushing aside her empty plate, he rumbled, "It seems your appetite has returned."

"You have no idea. It's so good to taste food again. Allie is a slave driver." She tipped her head to the side and lifted her brows. "I think I tried on everything Julian delivered."

He chuckled. "I had him order some things online." Cockily, he added, "I knew you'd stay."

She punched him playfully in the shoulder. "Right. Since you know everything now, how's Viv?"

"I just checked in with Jackson. She's adjusting well so far." Leaning against the bar, he lowered his voice to a whisper. "Your compulsion seems to be working."

Her face turned thoughtful. "Do you think she'll be okay if she comes tonight?"

He nodded. "Yes, she must swear fealty to join our Clutch. That will also happen this evening."

The head cook came by with a smile on her face. "Off with both of you. I have a million things to do in preparation, and I need my kitchen back."

Throwing his hands up in surrender, he grinned. "All right, Julie."

Viv

Slurping, I opened the door to see Sora hesitantly standing in the hallway. Slipping my fangs from the delicious bag of O neg, my eyes widened in surprise. "Hey!"

"Hey." She smiled. "Can I come in?"

I waved for her to come in and closed the door with my heel. "What brings you by, babe?"

She wrung her hands nervously. "I was just checking to see how you're doing."

Grinning, I took a quick inventory of how I felt. "Good, actually." A dreamy look stole over my face. "Jackson says I'm doing really well for a Fledgling."

Her sapphire eyes twinkled. "Ah, I see. I just bet he is."

My cheeks pinked. "Mmm hmm. Speaking of Fang Boys, you smell like Blaze."

She guffawed. "Fang Boys?"

Chuckling at my pun, I nodded. "Yup, just keeping it real." Tipping my chin, I wagged my brows. "So, Blaze?"

Blushing, she fidgeted. "Yes, we Mated."

A pang of jealousy went through my chest. Mated? What the hell?

Reading my stillness, she continued, "It's like this little voice inside me screaming 'mine' whenever I'm around him." She sighed. "I know I haven't really known him for long, but I just *know*."

I stopped listening when she said *mine*. Jackson elicited the same thought in me. I wanted him. Did he feel the same? Was it because he made me what I am? Rescued me from the hospital? Maybe it was just Stockholm syndrome or something.

A quick shove pulled me back to the moment.

Concerned, she snapped her fingers. "Hey, where'd you go?"

"I'm here, just trying to make sense of this." Turning, I tossed the bag into the trash and flopped onto my back on the bed.

Sora padded over and entered my view. "You know, I'm almost positive you have one too." Slyly, she added, "And, I know who it is."

Deciding to play along, I steepled my palms over my chest. "Oh really?"

She lifted a shoulder. "Maybe."

I kicked her playfully in the thigh.

Hopping up, she straddled my hips and began tickling my ribs in retaliation. Laughing, I cried, "Cheater, no fair!"

She stopped, and a knowing look stole across her face.

Damn it, she wanted me to say it. Covering my eyes, I peeked through my fingers. "Jackson."

Rolling onto her back, she stared at the ceiling. "Yup. I knew as soon as we got you home. All his ridiculous growling."

Raising up on one elbow, I queried, "Growling?"

"Yeah, the thought of Blaze changing you instead of him made him lose his shit," she laughed. "Blaze issued orders that all the"—she air quoted— "'Fang Boys' stay in the west wing before we Mated. He almost tore into Jackson when he startled me and I squeaked."

My chest rumbled at her words.

Hooking a thumb at my chest, she nodded. "Just like that."

Cutting off the sound, I tried to stuff away my protective instincts for a Vampire I barely knew and changed the subject. "What happens tonight?"

With a long sigh, she answered, "Well, it's a ball. I don't really know though. I guess it's like a Mating party and you swearing fealty to the Clutch all in one."

"A ball?" I asked incredulously. "Like fancy dresses and shit?"

She giggled. "Yeah."

Frustrated, I whined, "I don't have any clothes, Sora. All my crap was destroyed."

She patted my shoulder. "Hush. I'm sure Jackson will handle it. Blaze ordered a bunch of crap for me, so I have extras if you need them. You're taller now, so you should fit just fine. I had a mini fashion show with one of the" — she air quoted again — "'Fang Girls' a bit ago."

"Fang Girls? Yeah no, that includes us now." Curious, I asked, "How many are there?"

Somberly, she held up two fingers. "It's really difficult to make females. Blaze thinks the main reason we succeeded with you is because of my magic." Sora opened her palm, and her hand lit in a brilliant cobalt flame. The tips flickered playfully as they danced along her arm.

Awed by the display, I whispered, "It's really beautiful."

She smiled fondly. "Lay back and watch."

Once I'd settled against the pillows, she raised her hand toward the ceiling. An incredible silver light blossomed. Slowly, it morphed into shapes like a motion picture. A stairwell appeared. Jackson stormed into view, cradling me to his chest at the hospital. Next came Sora, healing me from her perspective. Gasping, I watched the wound on my hand close. She replayed my turning next, including a bit I hadn't remembered.

Abruptly, the light show cut off.

Softly, without meeting my eyes, she whispered, "You tried to attack me. Blaze restrained you and Jackson lost it. I have this weird ability and can place lasting compulsions on Vampires." Finally, she sorrowfully met my gaze. "I'm so sorry. I compelled you not to feed from anyone who wasn't willing, including me."

A beat later, I slapped her upside the head. "You're sorry?" I screeched. "What the hell is wrong with you? You did me a favor, idiot. Christ, woman, that's probably why I'm doing so well." Cocking my head, I smiled. "So, thank you."

She hesitated. "You're not upset?"

I smacked her again for her stupidity and elicited a full smile in return.

Her brows furrowed. "It needs to stay a secret that I can do that though, okay?"

Confused, I asked, "Why?"

She shrugged. "Only Masters are supposed to have that ability. Now that Blaze and I are Mated, it shouldn't be a big deal, but who knows?"

"Ah." A question formed in my mind. "What else can you do?"

"Weather, Water, Fire, Healing." She paused. "I can make wards that won't allow anyone who isn't invited to cross them."

I grinned. "That's pretty badass."

Tentatively, her lips lifted. "Thanks." Sitting up, she hopped from the bed. "I need some rest before this evening, and so do you. So, Sasha and Allie are coming by at six, to make me over. You want to come too?"

Eager to meet the other females, I nodded. "Sure. I'll see ya later."

Sora

Entering my room, Blaze's bass carried from the headboard. "How'd it go?"

"Really well," I sang.

He chuckled at my off-key notes.

"Hey, do you know if Jackson took care of getting clothes and stuff for Viv?"

"I reminded him earlier. He said he had it handled."

"Good," I answered, removing my clothes.

Appreciatively, he tracked my every movement. Patting the bed, he rumbled, "Come here."

Leaving the discarded garments on the floor, I joined him. Snuggled against his broad chest, he chastely kissed my forehead and flicked off the light.

A few minutes passed before I whispered, "Blaze?"

Grogginess colored his voice. "Yes?"

"Is the ward doing okay?"

Caressing the line of my spine, he chuckled. "Yes, Love, it's perfect. I would tell you otherwise. Now rest."

Satisfied with his answer, I hooked my leg over his and closed my eyes.

Jackson

Closing the door softly, he tried not to disturb her sleeping form. She looked so peaceful, the absolute opposite of her waking personality.

Quietly, he walked to the wingback. Leaning against it, he removed his boots, socks, and jeans. In his standard black tee and grey boxer briefs, he made his way to the other side of the bed and settled himself atop the covers.

Drowsily, she mumbled, "Jackson?"

"I'm here," he whispered.

Sighing, she rolled over and faced him. His enhanced sight roved her pale face, drinking in her high cheekbones, flawless skin, and pink, supple lips. The thick fan of her lashes lifted. Sky blue, the green flecks seemed to glow in the darkness. Her pink hair stuck out in wild tufts, making her look even more pixie-like.

With a vulnerable expression, she lifted a hand from below the blankets and reached hesitantly toward him. Catching her seeking fingers with his own, he ran his thumb across her open palm. Her lips curled as her lids lowered.

He watched her sleep for a long while, elated at the sensation of their joined hands.

Viv

The nightmare struck again. I knew it was a dream, but could not wake, nor change the events as they played out in terrifying detail.

A loud bang and the sounds of breaking glass woke me from a deep sleep. What the hell? Sitting up, I listened. The screech of metal rang out, sending my pulse skyrocketing.

Someone was downstairs in my shop. Grabbing my phone off the tiny, crooked nightstand, I stealthily slid from bed. Prying open the small wooden drawer, I grabbed my Ruger LC9 and flicked the safety off with my thumb.

Tiptoeing across the old wooden floors, I placed my weight where the boards wouldn't creak. Scanning the open hallway, I searched for any sign of movement.

Another scream of metal as it bent to its limit. Oh God, not the machines! Those things were expensive! Fuck!

My bare feet pounded down the hall toward the stairs leading to the shop below. A click-clack met my ears as I hit the first step.

Someone was coming up.

Unsure, I hesitated. Moving back the way I'd come, I kept my eyes trained on the stairs and lifted my gun.

Click, scrape, click, scrape, like a dog who wants to go outside. An animal? my mind stuttered.

Something was tearing; the sound was hollow like cloth being torn. A low growl rumbled.

Shifting my gun, I wiped the sweat from my palm onto the front of my tank. Everything fell silent except for the frantic beat of my heart.

"Turn around!" I screamed at my dream self. "Move!"

I backed up another step, and another growl came, only this one was behind me. Slowly, I turned.

Caught in the red glow of my alarm clock, amber eyes reflected from three feet above my bed. The second-story window, my mind supplied unhelpfully. I'd left it open.

Another rumble raised the hair on my arms as I pressed my spine against the wall to keep both entry points in view.

Click, click. A dark shape moved from the stairwell. The barrel of my gun trembled as I swung it from one target to the other.

My indecision cost me.

Before I could even process the squeak of the mattress, the amber-eyed thing sprang from the bed in an impossible leap and tackled me to the floor. My gun flew from my hand, clattering across the floor as warm saliva dripped down my cheek.

A sharp yip sounded from the stairwell. The huge beast above me slowly backed away in response.

Click, clack, click, clack. The sounds echoed in my skull as I could do nothing but watch, frozen in terror, as the thing made its way toward me. Huge white fangs inside an enormous maw flashed as it towered over me. I lifted a hand; in mercy or to ward it away, I didn't know. Quicker than I could track, its mouth opened and pierced my hand to the bone. I cried out once in surprise, then again in pain as my severed nerve endings registered the damage.

The agony centered my mind. I thumbed my phone to life, and the screen lit to reveal a massive brown Wolf. Golden eyes glared into mine as it dropped my arm like a chew toy. Snorting in my face, it turned away. The motion flashed a pink spot on its paw before it disappeared down the hall.

Thrashing came from my room as I cradled my injured hand to my chest.

Christ, it burned.

Wasting no time, I crawled to my tiny bathroom. Closing the door, I slid down its base. Flicking my cell back to life, I hit the emergency button on the screen. A thump rattled the door as the call connected.

"911, what is your emergency?"

A sob escaped my body and I started to shake…

"Shh, it's okay. Viv, Viv! Wake up!"

I was being physically shaken. Thank God.

A sob wracked my chest. "I'm h-here."

Corded arms gathered me to a firm chest as I inhaled a comforting scent. Jackson.

Repeatedly, he whispered, "I've got you, I've got you."

Eventually, my shudders subsided. Peace came and I drifted back to sleep in his embrace.

Jackson

He felt every sob, every tear as she clung to him like an anchor in a storm. When she finally calmed, he replayed her cries of fear and pain.

Mine… he swore.

As he held her smaller form, he decided he would teach her how to defend herself properly.

Then together, they would end the Pack.

He… the Clutch… and his Mate.

Janelle Peel

Chapter 12

Sora

Stepping out from the warm shower, I quickly wrapped myself in a plush navy towel. My feet chilled on the travertine floor as I debated whether to wear my hair up or down. It probably wouldn't matter, I mused. Allie and Sasha would be here soon to glam me up. Snatching another from the shelf, I twisted my locks into a turban.

Turning, I watched Blaze continue his shower with his eyes closed to the spray of mist. Individual drops gathered on his thick lashes. Slowly, they rolled down his cheeks to the edge of his perfectly sculpted jaw. I licked my lips, and my eyes continued their descent and traced every glorious muscle down to his narrow waist. His member hardened.

"Sora," he growled. "If you keep it up, we won't be going anywhere tonight."

I was caught, and my cheeks pinked. "Well maybe you should bathe alone or fully clothed from now on." Pivoting on my heel, I hit the switch to the waterfall and grabbed another towel. Shaking out the folds, I tossed it over the shower door and covered him from view.

Chuckling, he reached over and plucked it from the glass. With painstakingly slow movements, he worked it over the planes of his naked chest.

Huffing, I zipped to the closet before I could see his cocky grin.

Opening the massive mahogany doors, I pushed everything on the rack over and centered the teal dress in the open space.

Well, it was backless, so a bra was out. Good thing the girls were much perkier than before. Hmm, I probably couldn't wear panties either. A naughty grin curled my lips.

As I fingered the shimmering fabric, Blaze came up behind me. Trailing kisses from my shoulder to the shell of my ear, he whispered, "Do you like it?"

His breath raised goosebumps along my skin as I leaned against him. "It's lovely. I've never owned anything so amazing. Julian did well."

He nipped my lobe playfully. "Guess again."

Dropping the fabric, I turned and laced my fingers behind his neck. "You?"

Tipping his head, he brushed his nose against mine. "Mmm hmm, I hoped you'd wear it tonight."

Relaxing my hands, I traced the muscles from his neck to his pecs. Quickly, I undid my towel and pressed my bared form against him.

Groaning, he gripped my hips and pulled me closer.

I slid up his smooth torso, and my breasts rubbed against him as I stood on the tips of my toes. Running my fingers through his hair, I tipped my mouth to his lips. "Thank you." Mischievously, I wriggled out of his grasp and flashed to the bathroom. Giggling like a schoolgirl, I grabbed a robe from the hook in passing and entered the bedroom.

"Cheater!"

Grinning to myself as his chuckles echoed from the wardrobe, I slid the silver silk over my shoulders as a knock sounded.

"Just a sec!" I called, cinching the belt.

The air whispered as Blaze zipped between the door and me.

My thoughts scattered…

Inhale.

In a tux.

All Mother, he looked good enough to eat. His pressed black pants accentuated the perfect globes of his well-defined rear. The teal button-down shirt, tucked in at the waist, molded over his thick biceps. My mouth ran dry as I watched the corded muscles flex. Straining the seams, he tossed a dress jacket over one shoulder, with a bowtie dangling from his pinkie.

Taking in my stunned expression, he winked and opened the door. "Hey there. How are you feeling?"

Viv strode into the room in an emerald robe almost identical to my own with a plastic sheet covering her arm. Padding toward me, she stopped. Lifting her hand, she tapped my chin twice to shut my gaping mouth.

Janelle Peel

Turning, she snarked, "All right, Fang Boy. What the hell did you do to her?"

Throwing her a devious smirk, he exited.

Viv fanned my face. When that didn't elicit a response, she pinched my shoulder.

"Ow, Viv," I grimaced. "What the hell?"

"Hey." She waved. "Where the fuck were you?"

I patted my blushing cheeks, and a dreamy tone colored my response. "I've never seen him in a tux before."

"Oh." She cocked her head. "*Ohhhh*, did I interrupt something?" Wagging her brows, she pumped her hips to her own eighties porn music. "Bow chicka bow wow."

I giggled. "No. Sasha and Allie will be here any minute." Nodding to the thin plastic over her arm, I continued, "Did Jackson come through?"

The green flecks in her eyes sparkled in excitement. "Hell yeah he did!" Pivoting on her heel, she strode to the bed and laid out the garment bag.

Joining her, I motioned in a "get to it" gesture.

Bending, she slowly unzipped the plastic. Pausing dramatically, she revealed a shimmering turquoise gown.

Swallowing a gasp, I reached out to touch the plunging neckline.

Smack! She slapped my fingers with a playful smile. "Nope, not until I see yours."

Massaging the top of my reddened hand, I muttered, "Damn it, Viv."

She beamed as if enjoying my pain.

204

The sound of the door opening interrupted our antics.

Clutching two identical covers, Sasha's long mocha legs made short work of the distance to the bed.

Allie sidestepped her tall frame. "Hey, Sora."

Grinning, I hooked a thumb at the pixie beside me. "Hello, ladies. Meet my best friend, Viv."

Sasha wiggled her fingers. "So, you're the lovely thing that has Jackson MIA."

Viv blushed as Allie shushed the Amazonian beauty. "Hi, Viv. I'm Allie. Sasha is the loudmouth."

Sasha turned in mock outrage. "Me? Really? I don't think so." Rolling her sky-colored eyes, she tipped her chin to Allie. "No. This one has no filter."

Guffawing, Allie slapped a hand over her ample chest and tried to look abashed. "Truth."

Viv's eyes bounced back and forth between the bickering pair with a soft smile. "Well, it looks like I'm in good company then."

Chuckling, I mirrored Allie. "Truth."

Everyone laughed for a moment before Sasha broke up the party. "Well, girls, let's get to work. We only have about three hours to get us all dolled up."

Sobering, we got to it.

Hovering nervously by the entryway to the large staircase in the west wing, Allie patted my bare shoulder. "You look great, babe. I know it's kind of intimidating"—she waved toward the large gathering of people below us—"but you'll be fine. Trust me."

Viv stepped beside me with a grin. "Ready, bitch?"

Just breathe, I reminded myself. In and out.

Evidently, I was stalling a bit too long, so Viv smacked my butt.

Sasha giggled. "All right. Allie and I will go first. You two just follow after we hit the bottom step, okay?"

Gripping Viv's fingers, I nodded.

Out of view, we watched as they hit the first black carpeted stair.

Allie wore a pale green mermaid-style dress that expertly exposed her cleavage. I thought we'd never get her girls into the unforgiving fabric. The skirt trailed behind her in shimmering waves. Her riot of red curls was half up, half down, and was arranged to hide the strap of her halter. The gown's cut was similar to mine and bared the creamy white skin of her back before ending just above her rear.

Sasha towered over Allie and wore the same dress, only hers was a pastel blue that highlighted her kohl-rimmed eyes. Not much could be done with her short raven locks, so she wore diamond earrings that seemed to float just below her lobes. They in turn drew attention to her graceful neck. Open in the back, the gown showcased the play of muscles beneath her chocolate skin.

Both ladies had gone barefoot, as would Viv and I. They'd repeatedly assured me the floor was carpeted throughout the ballroom. I didn't want to freeze my freshly painted tootsies off. Fully into their second lives, the cold didn't bother them.

As they neared the last step, I looked at Viv. Her dress matched the emerald flecks in her turquoise irises. We'd managed to curl her short hair into soft waves atop her head. The effect created a softer pink than her normal spikes and contrasted brilliantly with the fabric of her gown. She chose Sasha's tiny diamond stud earrings because she didn't want to draw attention away from her small breasts. The dress fit like it was made for her. Its perfectly boned cups held her girls up and plunged to her waist.

Excitedly, she whispered, "Ready?"

Glancing back, I checked our trains to ensure they wouldn't trip us. I took her palm, and we padded toward the staircase.

Just breathe...

Blaze

He looked around as the members of his Clutch quieted. Allie and Sasha met their Mates at the bottom of the wide staircase.

Jackson stood beside him, clenching and unclenching his fists as he anxiously waited for Viv to appear.

Blaze quietly uttered, "Calm, Brother. This will be difficult, but you need to control yourself."

He'd informed the Clutch that Viv was Jackson's Mate, but they had yet to bond. Hopefully, they'd heed his words and not let their emotions get the best of them with a new female in the mix.

Jackson nodded as a few gasps and complete silence drew his attention back to the stairs.

Sora and Viv strode side by side from the hall.

Blaze skipped a cursory glance at Viv, but couldn't move his eyes from his Mate for long. Pure perfection. She inhaled a deep breath on the first step, straining the teal fabric wrapped around her pert breasts. Her oceanic eyes widened as she took in the crowd of over two hundred. Biting her lip, she skipped over the room until she found his gaze. The furrow of her brow softened. Exhaling, she smiled.

On the second step, her hips swayed with more confidence as he roved her body. The dress fit perfectly, he mused, lifting his lips to mirror hers. He'd had trouble finding a suitable gown, until Allie had come in at the right moment and helped him choose from the online site. She was right.

Shimmering with tiny crystals, it highlighted the silver tint of her hair and accentuated her lithe, hourglass figure. The skirt began just below the flare of her hips. Layered in sheer mesh, it covered her long legs before fanning out on the steps behind her. Silver, her toes sparkled.

A purr of appreciation began at the back of his throat. In response, her irises darkened to the color of sapphires. The bass of his purr deepened as he trailed over her bare shoulders and neck, fully displayed by the high twist of her curled locks.

Unable to contain himself, he met her on the fifth step, taking her delicate fingers in his own. Jackson followed and took Viv's.

"Hey," she whispered.

He rumbled, "Hello, Love."

Her cheeks pinked endearingly as he turned to the crowd. Lifting her hand up, he roared, "My Mate!"

Cheers and claps broke out as everyone assembled issued their support.

The sudden sound from the previously silent room must have startled Sora. Their joined hands lit in blue flames. Instantly, a hush settled over the crowd. A few members stepped forward to assist while some stepped back in fear.

Releasing Viv, Sora took a step back above Blaze on the staircase.

Blaze shifted their flickering grip higher, proving she could not harm him. He was her Mate.

The Clutch roared in approval while a few shook their heads at the scare.

Viv took Sora's arm and pulled her back down. "Shhh, it's fine."

As Sora's flames died, Blaze raised his palm for quiet. The crowd settled once more as he gestured to Viv.

Jackson held her hand up high. "Our newest member"—his voice carried across the room—"Viv!"

Cheers erupted once more as all four descended the steps and joined the party.

Blaze tipped his head. "Drinks?"

"Hell yes," Viv quipped.

Sora

I was overwhelmed by the sheer number of people introduced as we threaded our way to the bar on the back wall.

Blaze squeezed my hand reassuringly and bent his head to mine. "You're doing well."

His deep rumble trembled the small hairs inside my ear as we arrived at our destination. Witty as ever, I responded, "Whiskey, please."

Chuckling at my need for alcohol, he plucked a bottle from behind the bar while the bartender grabbed four rocks glasses.

Soft classical music slowly filtered through the air from one side of the room. Blaze poured and passed the half-full glasses to outstretched hands while I tried to calm my racing heart. So many faces, and I couldn't remember a single name.

I marveled at the large space, which was roughly the size of two gymnasiums. Black wall-to-wall carpet butted up against a slate tile dance floor in front of the small gathering of seated musicians. The walls matched the strategically placed marble pillars, white with silver reflective veins running through their tall lengths. A massive crystal and nickel chandelier hung in the center of the room with its lights twinkling merrily. Four wide shimmering teal panels hung from its thick chain and connected to each corner of the room. Stunningly, the wide bolts of fabric reflected the glittering light along the high ceiling.

Viv smacked her lips. "Damn that's good, Blaze."

I downed mine in one go and nodded for another. The burn helped to settle my nerves. "What's next?"

Jackson answered, "The Menagerie is amongst the guests. Any who wear a red cord around their bicep is available for feeding." My face screwed up in distaste. Throwing me a smirk, he continued in a patronizing tone, "Now, Sora, I know this is new for you, but it is our way of life. Try to accept that."

I shook my head, then shrugged my shoulders. "Whatever."

Blaze gave his brother a dirty look. "This night is for celebration. It will take some getting used to, I know." Hooking my waist with his free arm, he tipped his head to the corner opposite the band. "We also have hors d'oeuvres if you want anything. An hour from now, Viv will swear fealty to me and join our Clutch."

"Why doesn't Sora have to swear too?" Viv inquired curiously.

Confusion flashed across his face. "She's my Mate."

Cocking a brow, I quipped, "So, I get special treatment then?"

He grinned mischievously. "Always."

Cheeks pinking at his sexual innuendo, I shook my head. "If everyone else has done it, then I will too. We're all in this together."

Blaze took a deep breath. "Spoken like a true leader." He slapped his palm onto the bar. "It will be done."

Viv playfully punched him in the shoulder. "Good man. Now keep pouring, and let's dance!"

An hour later, I fidgeted by Viv on the third step of the grand staircase.

Blaze stood before us on the main level, facing the crowd. He lifted one heavily muscled arm into the air, and the room slowly quieted. His voice boomed to the crowd, "We are here to celebrate the addition of our newest members, Sora and Viv. Tonight, they swear fealty to our Clutch, to become one with our family."

As his words echoed throughout the room, every single person took a knee and bent their heads in one massive wave.

A sniffle beside me caught my attention. Viv had tears pooling in her eyes. Reaching out, I took her hand in mine and squeezed once in silent question.

Softly, she whispered, "I'm okay. I just haven't had a family in so long."

My beautiful, strong-willed friend. I loved her more in that moment than ever before. Tipping my chin, I placed a soft kiss on her brow. She gripped my fingers tighter in appreciation.

Blaze turned to us with a happy smile on his face as he bowed. We answered his movement with a curtsy of our own. Standing tall once more, he motioned us toward him. Our bare feet made no sound as we descended the steps one last time.

Jackson came forward with an aged gold chalice and placed it into his brother's open hand before stepping back.

With a snick of his fangs, Blaze pierced the flesh of his palm. The scent of his blood caused my stomach to rumble.

Suppressing a grin at my reaction, he dribbled a few ruby drops into the chalice. Sealing the punctures, he held the cup out to me.

I released Viv, and my fangs dropped as I took his offering. Piercing my skin, I mirrored him and gave the cup to Viv.

Blinking hard, she repeated our motions and passed it back to Blaze.

Blaze swirled the liquid before facing the room. He boomed, "Now we join. One family!"

His shouted words were repeated in whispers around the room.

"One Clutch!"

The words echoed with more volume as everyone rose.

"May the next part of your journey be more fruitful than the first." Blaze raised the cup to his lips and took a small drink. Turning, he gestured to the crowd. "As they have joined with me, now shall you." Gently, he settled the chalice in Viv's open hand.

She drank and handed it to me.

"Ours," I growled vehemently before taking my own sip. Blaze nodded his approval at my rumbled outburst as the last drops trickled down my throat.

Mine... a voice whispered.

Blaze

Sora's growl reverberated throughout the room and an intense feeling of pride overcame him. Yes, she was a worthy Mate indeed. Strong, fierce... *His.*

Applause broke out as she lifted the chalice from her lips and passed it back to Jackson.

"My family!" she shouted to everyone in attendance. "*Mine.*" Her exposed fangs glistened in the twinkling light. She raised her palm, and her azure flames ignited. As she threw out her arm toward the chandelier, Blaze turned to watch her magic race from her outstretched fingers in an arcing light.

BOOM!

The chandelier shattered into tiny glowing specks as everyone hit the floor but him.

Where the fixture had been, a brilliant orb began to take shape. It pulsed with more power than he had ever seen.

Janelle Peel

"Mine," her whisper carried throughout the silent room on a powerful breeze.

The sphere glowed orange as it rotated. Quickly it grew to the size of a small car. Faster it spun, round and round. Finally, it settled and lit the darkened room. Smaller red flares licked across its surface. It was as bright as the sun, he marveled, feeling the heat as the flames coiled around it.

She screamed as the gathered crowd stood. "I walk in daylight! Tonight, you will too!"

Everyone raised their faces and basked in the warm glow. Slowly they turned toward him as she tucked herself against his side.

"Ours," she purred, meeting his gaze. Small stars glittered inside her sapphire depths.

"Ours," he whispered back in agreement.

Bending at the waist, he swept her off her feet and cradled her close in the crook of his arms.

Awed whispers sounded behind him.

"Daywalker."

"Dhampir."

"Mage."

"Chosen."

Applause broke out as he carried her up the stairs and back to their room.

214

Chapter 13
Viv

Well, *that* was interesting.

The sphere continued to pulse and flare after my friend's abrupt outburst and subsequent absence. The soft notes of a violin slowly filled the air, and the murmurs of voices continued once more.

I panned the room in search of Jackson. He owed me a dance. On my third scan, I spotted him threading his way back toward the bar.

Nodding politely to the whispers of congratulations ringing in my ears, I stalked my prey.

At my arrival, he slid two half glasses of whiskey forward and passed one to my open hand.

"So..." I drew out.

Sipping, he lifted a brow. "So?"

I waved at the ceiling. "This kind of thing happen often?"

He chuckled. "No. We have a Mage, but never has she recreated the sun. Her talents lie more in healing and warding."

"Ah, I see. Where is she anyway?"

He sighed, his shoulders rounding. "On sabbatical." He gestured vaguely. "Every so often she leaves us to regroup and improve her magic, etcetera."

Taking in his posture, I quipped, "What, she your girlfriend or something?"

"No," he bit out. "Things would just be easier if she were here."

Swallowing my whiskey, I pondered his reaction. Weird moody Vampire. He could keep his secrets.

Bored with the topic, I touched his forearm. "Would you like to dance?"

He eyed me down the line of his nose. "I don't dance."

"Everyone dances," I cajoled. "It's just a matter of how well they dance."

Allie stepped up beside me. "He really doesn't. I've been here for quite a while and I've never seen him bust a move." She rocked her hips in a side-to-side motion and threw her arms up. Her large breasts jiggled precariously with the movement.

Grinning, I tipped my crown to her chest. "Careful there, you might lose one of the girls."

She laughed and hooked my shoulders. "I'll dance with you." Her nose scrunched. "But not to this. Sasha and I were heading to the rec room. There's a stereo there, full bar, pool table; anything you could want." Her brows lifted hopefully. "Want to come?"

That was the best idea I'd heard all night. "Sounds good. I can play a mean game of nine ball, or anything with balls." I smirked at my pun.

Allie giggled.

I glanced at Jackson. His face was an emotionless mask while he continued to nurse his drink. I shrugged. "Let's go."

We found Sasha kissing Jake goodbye near the stairs.

Allie lopped her arm through Sasha's while we watched Jake retreat through the side door. "Duty calls?"

Sasha sighed. "Yeah, some more of the Pack have been sighted sniffing around the perimeter."

"I know, they called Von in right after we got here. Stupid Pack. I can't wait until all of this is over and things go back to normal."

Snapping my fingers in front of their faces, I asked, "What's normal? New girl, fill me in."

"Drinks," they replied in unison.

Sasha grabbed my wrist. "Come on."

While Allie fiddled with the massive sound system, I racked the pool balls for a game of cutthroat.

Sasha hovered behind the bar. "What's your poison, Viv?"

"I was drinking whiskey," I replied, joining her.

Her lips lowered in disgust. "That's nasty. Vodka it is."

I chuckled. "I'll drink whatever you're pouring." Sobering, I continued, "So, what's happening with the perimeter?"

Sasha flared her nostrils in irritation as she began pouring shots. "Well, we used to be able to go out at night and do as we please. Now, though, we're on lockdown. We have to stay inside the ward. The Pack is trying to provoke a war over Sora." She lifted her hands. "Don't get me wrong, Sora is awesome. We love having her here; we love that Blaze has found his Mate. But we've been cooped up inside the mansion, and our Mates are patrolling so much we hardly see them. I don't know what they want from Sora"—she shook her head—"but she could be a dangerous weapon if they ever got their hands on her."

I nodded. I could see that. She was incredibly powerful. Her magic was extraordinary. I had a feeling she was just barely scratching the surface of her power.

AC/DC's "Back in Black" came on over the speakers as Allie settled onto a stool. "Sasha's right. The whole situation sucks ass. I just wish the Pack would go away."

My thoughts turned back to my first encounter with the Pack, and I shivered.

Intuiting my discomfort, Allie touched my cheek softly. "Sorry to bring up bad memories, babe."

I shook off the negative emotions and downed my vodka. The burn was a bit harsher than the aged whiskey, but it still tasted damn good. "Another, Sasha," I said, sliding my empty toward her. "I'm going to beat your asses at a game of cutthroat." A mischievous smile lit my face. "Who's breaking?"

After the eighth game of me kicking their butts, we decided to call it quits.

Putting away her cue, Sasha shook her head. "Where the hell did you learn to play like that?"

Shrugging, I adopted a bland voice. "I lost my parents when I was seven in a car accident. From there, I bounced around group homes. There was always a pool table, and we'd gamble amongst each other for extra food."

Both Allie and Sasha flashed toward me and crushed me between them in a Viv sandwich.

"We're your family now," Allie whispered in my ear while Sasha rubbed my shoulder soothingly.

My eyes teared up for the second time that night. I took a deep breath, and my tone turned reedy. "I know. That Wolf attack was terrifying, but it's a small price to pay to be here." Sniffling, I mustered a smile as they stepped back to examine me.

A knock in the hall preceded Jackson as he stepped into the room. "Am I interrupting?"

Getting control of myself, I turned to face him. "No, we're just reminiscing. What's up?"

His face softened in concern for a moment before his mask slid back into place. "Well, if you're finished here for the evening, I have something I'd like to show you."

I looked to Allie and Sasha.

They bobbed their heads.

"Okay. I'll see you girls later?"

Allie smiled. "Sure, we're here every night. Come find us and we'll try nine ball."

Sasha beamed. "Hopefully, I can beat you at that."

Following Jackson, I snarked over my shoulder, "Don't count on it!"

Their giggles followed me out of the room.

I caught up with Jackson after we entered the second kitchen. "Where are we going?"

Silently, he opened a large steel door with a metal bar leaning against its frame.

"The training grounds," he replied. At my quizzical expression, he gestured for me to hurry up.

Sighing at his ever-changing moods, I stepped over the threshold. Rough concrete met my bare feet as I looked down a flight of stairs. Geez. The walls were made of reinforced steel like some creepy horror movie.

Jackson secured the door with a deep thud and descended the steps with practiced ease.

In for a penny, in for a pound I guess. Lifting the skirt of my dress, I trailed after him.

The stairs ended at the beginning of a long tunnel comprised of more steel and concrete. Yup, I mused. Definitely a horror movie.

It was eerily quiet. I hazarded we were deep underground. I rolled my eyes at his silence as we trekked on for what seemed like forever.

Finally, we reached another steel door. Jackson turned the handle, held it open, and jerked his head for me to enter.

Once inside, I took in the small chamber. The only change was a black bench off to the side and a rebar ladder leading up through a tube to God knew where.

I looked at Jackson curiously.

He pointed. "Up."

What a jackass.

The rungs were cold on my bare feet as I tried not to trip over the hem of my gown. Grumbling to myself, I stepped into a deserted room with bunks lined up in tidy rows.

Jackson passed me again and led me to the other side of the room. Yet another steel door greeted us. Yippy.

I clenched my teeth in annoyance as he pulled it open and I entered.

Wow, my eyes widened as I stopped to stare at the huge room. It reminded me of one of those fancy "members only" gyms.

Workout equipment took up half of the real estate, with colorful rock-climbing pegs drilled into the abutting grey wall. A small catwalk circled the three-story space. Ropes hung overhead at varying lengths and intervals from the ceiling. The other half of the floor was made up of a red dojo-style mat, complete with a weapons rack bristling with everything from wooden training swords to javelins. Guns, machetes, even a battle ax, all hung from the black hooks in orderly rows.

My lips formed an *O* as I spied a shooting range tucked away in the corner by another door. What the hell? Training grounds, indeed.

The sound of the door settling into place snapped my mouth shut with a click.

Jackson moved to sit on a weight bench near the other equipment and began unlacing his shiny dress shoes. Standing, he toed them off. Shucking his blazer, he revealed a green dress shirt that strained to contain the sinewy muscles of his arms.

Turning away, I watched him from the corner of my eye when he finally spoke.

"There's a black bag next to you." He paused to pull his bowtie free. "The clothes should be your size. The locker room is over there by the range."

I followed the jerk of his head as he began working the buttons free from his shirt.

Not wanting to stay and stare more than I already had, I picked up the small pack from the arm of the treadmill. Opening it, I walked to the locker room. Hmm, I thought, pawing through the bag.

The room was as big as my bedroom. Charcoal-painted lockers took up one wall, with toilet stalls on the other. White plastic curtained showers were lined up at the end of the room. Catching my reflection as I passed the mirror above the utilitarian sinks, I flashed myself a thumbs-up.

Placing the bag on the hook in the first stall, I unlatched the clasp under my arm and slowly slid the hidden zipper down to my hip so I wouldn't get pinched. My breasts sprang free as the shimmering turquoise material slipped down my frame and pooled at my feet. Lifting the gown from the floor, I threw it over the curtain rod.

What I'd failed to notice with my cursory glance of the bag's contents, now became blaringly clear. No sports bra, no panties. The panties weren't a worry, but my small C's would feel every bump and jostle if we were going to work out. Smirking to myself, I pulled the tank over my head and wondered what Jackson's reaction would be.

The top fit like a second skin and showcased the outline of my nipples beneath the black fabric. Adjusting the thin shoulder straps to display some cleavage, I pulled on the stretchy yoga pants and nearly fell over as my foot caught in the leg.

Real smooth, Viv.

Exiting the stall, I checked my reflection.

Not too shabby! Everything molded perfectly to my body. The pants flared slightly from my knee to my ankle. A bit long, but not as bad as they would have been had I not gained six inches in height when I was turned.

Taking a deep breath, I went to find Jackson.

Jackson

Standing in the center of the rubber mat, he tried to calm his nerves as the door to the locker room swung open.

Viv snarked as she approached, "Okay. I've dressed appropriately. Now, tell me what the hell we're doing."

He grinned at her fiery tone. "Practice. You need to learn your new skillset. How fast you can move, how to take someone down." Pausing, he lowered his voice. "How to kill."

She cocked a hip. "I suppose you think you can show me how to do that?"

He chuckled. "Yes."

Sarcasm laced her reply. "Mmm hmm, right." She waved toward the weapons rack. "Swords? Grappling? Martial arts?"

Smirking, he rumbled, "Lady's choice."

Her hips swayed as she approached him. The cotton of her tank accentuated every delicate curve of her figure. He sucked in a breath when he noticed she wasn't wearing anything beneath his selections.

"Yeah," she quipped, "didn't quite think this through, did ya?"

The emerald flecks in her dark eyes sparkled in merriment as she gave him her own perusal. Beginning at his bared feet, she took in his dress pants and slowly worked her gaze up before ending at his naked chest. Inhaling in short bursts, she took in his scent.

He cleared his throat. "Apologies. I don't dress women often."

Her face turned predatory as her pupils dilated.

Confused, his brow furrowed.

She rumbled, "Dress women occasionally, then?" Blurring her frame, she slammed him to the mat. Pinning his arms above his head, she straddled his waist. Glaring, she bit out, "Good enough?"

Grinning, he flipped her beneath him. Leaning down to her exposed ear, he whispered, "No."

She shifted her hips and threw him over her head. Standing, she flashed to the weapons rack and grabbed a wooden staff.

Taking her challenge, he padded over and chose his own pole. Pacing back to his original position, he curled his fingers into a "give it your best shot" motion.

Zipping toward him, he tried to anticipate her swing.

Thwack!

The pole thudded behind his knees and dropped him to his back once more. Looming over him, she leisurely tapped the blunt end of her staff against his neck. "Not good enough. Try again."

His foot shot out to trip her before she could move back. She stumbled, but refused to fall. Her pole almost punctured the rubber a hair's breadth from where his head had been. He zipped to the other side of the ring as she straightened. She twirled her long stick with deft fingers, and a challenging gleam entered her eyes. Balancing on the balls of her feet, she curled her fingers.

He flashed to strike her thigh.

Thunk!

The sound echoed off the concrete walls. He felt the reverberation of his strike on her pole instead. Stepping back, he nodded in approval.

Faster than he could track, she feinted toward his right knee. He fell for it. She brought the other end of her staff up in one smooth motion and slammed it under his chin.

Blood dribbled from his mouth as he bounced twice on the rubber mat. How had she bested him?

Eyes twinkling in silent laughter, she leaned against her pole and offered her hand.

Viv
This was fun!

Jackson reached toward my outstretched fingers. The corner of his right eye tightened. Intuiting his intent as his hand grasped mine, I braced my legs while he flexed his torso to pull me down.

Then I let go.

Standing my full five-foot-six height, I chuckled as he fell back again. Swaying my hips, I sauntered away. "Nice try."

Growling, he got to his feet and spit a mouthful of blood onto the mat.

Mine…

I flashed toward him and tackled him. Slowly, I licked the ruby liquid staining his lips. Delicious; salty and masculine.

More, a voice whispered.

Wait, what? Forcing myself back to the moment, I lifted my hips and snarked to cover my animalistic response, "Don't be wasteful." Turning away, I replaced my staff in the rack. "What's next?"

He stood. The evidence of my reaction was clear in the tenting of his pants. He'd liked it.

I smirked at his predicament. "Hmm?"

Padding over, he placed his staff next to mine. With a vulnerable expression, he took in my smaller form from head to toe. "Why did you do that?"

My brows scrunched as I evaded, "What? Drop you? You have a tell, the corner of your right eye tightens when you're trying to be sneaky."

He shook his head, knowing full well that I wasn't answering his question. Changing tactics, he asked, "What else can you do?"

"I'm not really sure. Grappling and fighting with broom handles was the extent of my physical interaction with the other kids at the orphanage." Pausing, I remembered the reason I had to learn to fight. My tiny frame marked me as prey to the older boys when the lights went out. Shrugging out of the memory, I swallowed the bile rising in the back of my throat.

Sympathy reflected in his gaze as he reached out to grab my hand.

Shifting away, I angrily grasped a steel sword hilt instead. I wasn't weak, and I sure as hell didn't want anyone's pity.

He dropped his arm and sighed. "Talk to me."

"No," I replied hotly, unsheathing the three-foot length. The metal sang. "Let's try this instead."

Shaking his head, he moved out of reach. "I want to train you, Viv, I do, but not like this." Turning away, he walked toward the bench where he'd left his clothes.

"Fine, fucking leave then," I yelled after him. "I don't owe you anything."

In a flash of movement, he was gone.

During the entire hour that followed, I berated myself. He was only trying to be nice, and I'd let my old hurts shut him out.

Swinging effortlessly from the ropes above the catwalk, I dared myself to take needless risks to escape the hurricane of emotions.

Evidently, I took one too many. Releasing the cord in my hand, I stretched to grasp the shorter rope instead of the easy one within reach. I gasped as it slid through the tips of my outstretched fingers.

Falling twenty-five feet to the floor below, I braced for impact.

Craaack!

My right forearm snapped. The sound echoed in my ears before the pain could register.

Mother fucker!

Cradling the injury against my belly, I rocked up to stand. Tears streamed down my cheeks. Stupid, stupid! I knew better! What the hell was wrong with me?

I angrily stomped on the floor for two steps before the tantrum jostled my arm.

Screaming once in agony, I took a breath and resolved to suffer in silence.

Exiting the gym, I moved through the barracks.

Shit! How the fuck was I going to get down the ladder? It had to be dawn by now. Sliding to the floor by the tube, I tried to figure out a plan, when I heard someone coming up.

Black hair poked out first. Striking blue eyes pierced mine as a male came fully into view. Wiry shoulders and a narrow waist made an appearance next as he stepped out of the tube.

I waved the fingers of my opposite hand and attempted a smile. "Hi."

Brow furrowing, he took a knee and inspected my injury. A scarlet line trickled down my elbow. His mouth formed an O at the sight of the exposed bones.

Hiding behind my snark, I quipped, "I'm Viv, and you are?"

"Mason." He tipped his head. "I lead the Protectors. Can I help you back to your room? It's daylight, so we'll have to use the tunnel."

I sighed in relief. "Pleased to meet you, Mason. And, yes, that would be splendid."

Mason stood. Climbing three steps down the ladder, he motioned for me to place myself in front of him. I did as he requested and leaned against his hard frame as my bare feet found each rung. It was slow going, but way better than trying to do it on my own.

After we reached the chamber below, he carefully scooped me up into his strong arms. Effortlessly, he carried me through the tunnel almost as fast as a Vampire.

Making our way through the house to my room, he paused at the door. My bloodied fingers turned the handle, and he shouldered his way inside.

One moment I was secure in his arms, the next I was rudely dropped to the floor. My arm shrieked in pain and I cried out. Gritting my teeth, I looked around to figure out what the hell happened.

Jackson had Mason pinned against the floor with his fangs bared menacingly above his throat.

"Jackson!" I screeched. Flinging out a foot, I kicked him in the face and knocked him from Mason.

Flashing, I crouched over my Clutchmate protectively. My fangs dropped and I hissed a warning.

Jackson rocked back on his ass with a curious expression as his canines retracted. Clearing his throat, he took in my arm. "What's going on?"

Pissed, I growled.

Jackson stood. Turning his back to me, he padded to the wingback and sat.

After a few moments of silence with his face shuttered, I relaxed. My teeth snapped back into place. Blood ran down my skin. It dripped onto Mason's hip with a wet splat. Keeping Jackson in my periphery, I glanced down.

Mason opened his eyes and stared at the door frame. "Will there be anything else, Miss Viv?"

Flabbergasted by his formality and nonchalance at what had transpired, I stood and stepped aside.

Mason got to his feet as I sucked in a breath to answer his question. "No, Mason. It was a pleasure meeting you. I'm soooooorry," I drew out, glaring at Jackson, "you had to go through that. Thank you for helping me back to—" I paused and raised my voice "—MY ROOM, after I injured myself."

Jerking a nod, he retreated as quickly as possible.

I bared my teeth at Jackson.

Splat.

Splat.

Splat.

Jackson stared at me.

I rumbled a challenge at him.

Sighing, he lowered his eyes. Slowly, he stood and walked to the mini fridge in the corner. Pulling out a blood bag, he padded toward me and held it out. Still looking at the floor, he softly asked, "Can I look at your arm, please?"

Saliva pooled in my mouth as I snatched the bag. In a blink, I punctured the plastic. Drinking, I moaned my consent.

Gingerly, he lifted my elbow from my chest. I whimpered as the protruding bones ground together.

"Shh, shh, just a moment. Everything will be fine," he soothed while guiding me to the bed. "I'm just going to go next door so Sora can have a look."

Grabbing a pillow as I sat back, he gently placed it under my jacked-up arm.

I slurped faster as the pain shocked through me.

He moved toward me in reassurance.

I bared my teeth. Asshole.

Backing away, he held up his hands. "Okay, okay. I'll be right back."

In a flash, he was gone. The mahogany panel slowly started to swing closed. Just before the latch clicked, Sora barreled into the room wearing nothing but a silver robe.

Jackson and Blaze trailed in after her.

Briefly, she assessed my injury, then barked, "Leave us!"

Blaze turned on his heel and snagged Jackson's shoulder while he hesitated.

"But," Jackson began. He didn't get a chance to finish as Blaze physically lifted him and tossed him into the hall. Tugging the door closed behind him, he followed Sora's orders without a backward glance.

I swallowed the last dregs of the bag and tossed it onto the nightstand. "Hey."

Her black eyes sparked with silver stars as her fangs descended with a click. "What the fuck happened?" She was pissed.

I raised my good arm placatingly. "Calm down. It was an accident. I hurt myself." Grudgingly, I added, "Jackson wasn't even there."

She growled in frustration, "How?"

My upper lip lifted in disgust. "We were at the training grounds. Shit got too heavy and I snapped at him. He left. I felt like an ass, so I took it out on my body. I fell from a rope above the catwalk." Flaring my nostrils, I gritted my teeth. "Okay, Mom?"

She tutted for a moment. Smirking, her canines retracted. "You are an ass, Vivian."

My face lit in embarrassment. "You swore you would never use that word!"

Giggling, she settled herself on the mattress near my wound. "I know, but you deserved it." She paused, her face turning remorseful. "This might hurt, or…"

I waved my hand. "Or?"

Her brow lifted. "Or I could compel you to sleep, then try to fix it."

"What the hell do you mean, try?"

She rolled her eyes. "I have magic, Viv. It's NEW. Or you can try to set the bone and wait for your Vampire healing to take over while you rest."

I was already shaking my head. "Nope. No thanks. You set it, you heal it, no compulsion. I've had broken bones before."

She tipped her head to the visible pieces of my ulna and radius. "That's two bones, without painkillers."

I growled, "Just do it."

Faster than I thought possible, she jerked my arm out, straightened the bones, and slapped her other hand over the ragged hole in my arm.

The pain hit.

An agonized scream began at the back of my throat as a healing warmth coated the area and instantly provided relief.

Sagging into the pillows, I watched the white glow of her power flare across my skin. "God, that feels amazing."

She smiled softly and continued working her magic.

A few minutes later, the light dimmed.

Lifting my arm, I flexed my fingers.

She squealed and clapped her hands. "Good as new!"

My smile turned into a yawn as I tried and failed to thank her.

Standing, she patted my shoulder. "You should rest. If there's anything left to heal, your body will take care of it while you sleep." Padding to the door, her silver robe swished with the movement until she stopped with her hand on the handle. "Should I let Jackson in? He was really worried when he busted in on us."

My jaw cracked as another yawn overtook my mouth. Rolling over, I mumbled, "Whatever."

Janelle Peel

Chapter 14

Sora

As I closed the door, Jackson flashed toward me from the end of the hall and slammed into Blaze like a brick wall. Snickering, I peeked around a well-muscled bicep. "She's fine, Jackson. Calm down."

Taking a deep breath, the anxiety lining his forehead relaxed. "Sorry, I was worried."

Blaze placed a reassuring hand on his arm. "Have you told her?"

Jackson's shoulders slumped in defeat. Tucking his chin, he stared at the carpet. "I don't know how."

What? He didn't know how? Almost a millennium old, and he didn't know how to talk to a woman? What. The. Fuck. I snapped, "She knows, you idiot. Quit screwing around. She won't open up to you, so either grow a sack and talk to her, or leave her alone and let her come to you." Pausing, I bared my teeth. "You pushed her at the Training Grounds, didn't you?

Then you left her there when you didn't get the answers you wanted. Everyone leaves her, you idiot. What is wrong with you?" Irritated, I started pacing. "She's had a rough life. She's strong, but if she gets hurt, I will hurt you." Rounding on him, I slapped my open palm onto his chest and growled protectively. "Are we clear? She is *mine* as are *you*."

Jackson immediately dropped to one knee as my power uncoiled. It lashed the air with invisible whips of anger.

"Apologies, Mistress. I will try my best to take care of it."

I stopped. My mouth opened and closed like a fish. "Mistress?" I whispered, then shrieked at Blaze, "I am not your whore!"

Blaze chuckled. Nodding to his brother's submissive form, he met my gaze. "It's not what you think."

I glared.

He threw up his hands. "We originate from a time where the feminine word for Master is Mistress. A concubine, however, is what Mistress means in today's society." He smirked. "Would you prefer Madam? Lady, perhaps?"

My brows furrowed at the new information. I debated the options for a moment. Madam was old, like a spinster sister with cats, maybe even a brothel owner. Lady seemed naive, like a young single woman of nobility, or some virgin-like crap. "Fine," I muttered, "but I want to see a dictionary, damn it."

Blaze full out laughed at my naïveté.

Jackson's shoulders shook as he tried to contain himself.

My ears turned red. "All right, jerks, enough." I sliced my hand through the air. "Jackson, go. Make this right."

He stood and fidgeted. "Yes…"

"Sora, or Mistress." I threw my hands up in exasperation. "What the fuck ever." Storming to my room, I slammed the door.

Fuming, I paced a line in the plush carpet. What little shits! Hello, it was the twenty-first century. Bastards.

Slipping off my robe, I tossed it onto the wingback and settled in bed. If I was truly honest with myself, Mistress did sound kind of cool. Plus, all the other Vampires would know what it meant, Master and Mistress. Yes, I tapped my fingers on my chin, that could work. I just hated how dirty it sounded.

Blaze entered. Clearing his throat to make sure I was listening, he rumbled, "I should have explained. I apologize. This is a first for me. I didn't even think of how the Clutch would address you." Beaming, he slipped off his grey pajama pants. "Plus with your reaction at the fealty ceremony…"

As his words trailed off, I did a play-by-play of my emotional state at the ceremony. I felt welcomed, like this was the home I'd been searching for. Sipping from the chalice every Clutch member's blood stained… I felt their power filter through me. It was heady and euphoric. They were my family. *Mine*. I would die to protect them.

Janelle Peel

I voiced part of my thoughts. "Would you die for them, any of them?"

"Yes, every single one."

I pressed further. "You would give them anything within reason. They are your home, your life, your family?"

His pupils overrode the normal cobalt of his irises. "Yes. But that was before I met my Mate. I would still do anything for them, but my emotions will likely cloud my judgement regarding you."

Satisfied, I sighed. "Me too."

His brows dipped in question. "Why the mini sun?"

How to explain it… My nose scrunched. "When was the last time you saw it? Felt its rays kiss your skin?"

Softly, he heartbreakingly whispered, "Almost a millennium, Love. It was beautiful."

My voice rumbled into an appreciative purr. "They are *mine*, like you are *mine*. My family. The words needed to describe what I felt escape me." I opened and closed my arms. "Why not give them something they have yearned for, when they have given me what I have sought for so long?"

His face softened. "You are perfect. A strong leader, healer; everything I could ever have hoped for in a Mate, and so much more. My equal in every way." He touched my cheek. "I love you with all that I am, all that I ever will be, and more every single day."

Shifting my position, I leaned up to his tall frame and palmed his cheeks. "I love you too."

A single tear trickled down his cheek at my admission.

Then he kissed me.

Jackson

He paced outside the room for quite some time before he worked up the courage to enter.

Seeing Viv curled on the bed in slumber, he sighed. He wasn't sure if that was good or bad.

Quietly, he undressed to his boxer briefs and crawled beneath the duvet. Viv tossed and turned in her sleep. He reached over to wake her, but lowered his hand indecisively, unsure of his welcome.

Lying back, he replayed all his encounters with her. She was strong, but fragile. Things had to be on her terms. Confronting her as he had was a mistake, one he hoped she'd let him rectify soon.

She thrashed a hand out and mumbled, "No."

He clasped her fingers inside his own. She settled for a moment, then rolled her tiny frame over and laid her head upon his chest. He purred at the sensation.

She snuggled closer and looped a leg over his thigh. Sighing softly, she quieted.

As he breathed in her unique scent, he drifted off with her.

Blaze

Sora bolted upright and cried out in pain, "Ow!"

Instantly on alert, he wrapped an arm around her and scanned the darkened room for intruders. Finding none, he rumbled, "What is it?"

She pressed a hand to her chest. "Shit, that hurts." After rubbing her sternum for a moment, she sucked in a sharp gasp. "The ward!"

His phone started to ring. He flashed to it before the first tone could end.

Mason sent a group text, 'Security breach, the Ward has been weakened. All available personnel are to report immediately to the barracks.'

"Fuck!" He zipped from the bed to the wardrobe and dressed in his fatigues faster than humanly possible.

Sora was just pulling on a black tank as he rushed by to get his boots.

"Blaze," she whispered, reaching toward him as her head poked through the neckline.

He instantly stopped at her worried tone. "Yes?"

Her wide blue eyes displayed fear as she uttered, "It's still daylight."

They sped soundlessly through the tube a moment later. Blaze nearly jerked the door from its hinges in frustration as he opened it for Sora.

She placed a palm on his chest and whispered, "Shh, I've got this." Then she was gone. The rustle of her pants was the only sound he heard of her zipping up the rebar rungs.

He took a deep breath and counted to five. Slowly, he released it through his clenched teeth and followed her.

"Report!" Sora's commanding voice met his ears as he exited the tube.

Thirty Protectors filled the space with their heads bowed.

Mason knelt before Sora while Blaze moved to stand at her back. "Mistress, forgive me. We are still investigating. An explosion drew one of our roving patrols to the eastern perimeter. So far, the ward is holding. However, the fence line has been blown apart." He sucked in a breath. "There was no scent of an incendiary device. It has to be magic."

Blaze growled in frustration. The rumbles echoed off the steel-reinforced walls.

Sora turned toward him as her cobalt eyes sparkled in the artificial light. Her growl of disapproval met and exceeded his own. "Ours."

Sora

Blaze nodded his agreement.

I turned to Mason. "Has Jackson been informed?"

He addressed the floor. "Yes, Mistress. He has yet to respond."

My tone sharpened. "No more announcements, texts, or calls to the Clutch. I will not tolerate anyone else being put in danger. Show me."

Mason stood. Glancing briefly at Blaze, he led me to the door and out into the fading afternoon light.

Zipping across the field of green grass, I wondered at all the possibilities before coming to the only conclusion available. It had to be the Council. Sure, the Pack had a Mage, but I quickly dismissed the idea entirely. My magic was stronger. Why else would their Alpha want my help?

Broken thoughts flitted through my mind as we arrived at the ward just before a large hole in the fence. It appeared deserted, but something made the small hairs rise on the back of my neck.

I scanned the perimeter; not a soul was in sight. Slowly, I crouched. Lowering my hand into the soil, I reached toward the ward. In my mind's eye, I could see where the silver strand of the previous ward had been, but it was gone entirely. My blue still shimmered as strongly as when I'd first laid it, but the red lines accompanying it with Blaze's feeding were gone. Odd.

Finished with my assessment, I stood. The feeling of being watched increased as goosebumps broke out along my skin. Growling, I dropped into a fighting stance. "Who's there?"

A single figure stepped into view two hundred yards away. I sniffed in futility and noted the person was downwind.

Khaki pants outlined curved hips with a hot-pink cropped polo as the woman strode closer. Strutting along with a confident swagger, she wore low-heeled, knee-high leather boots. Auburn hair kissed a round face paired with green eyes and an upturned nose.

I sucked in a shocked gasp and cut off my growling. "Daisy?"

She stopped, her expression lighting with confusion. Taking a single step closer to the fence, she called out, "Sora?"

We stared at each other as we had many times before. I hadn't seen her in ages. I cocked a hip, and she mirrored the movement.

Incredulous whether this was indeed my childhood playmate, I asked, "What are you doing here?"

Her eyes lit in comprehension and she tipped her head to the side. "Finally came into your own?" She waved a hand at the ward. "Your work?"

My face shuttered. Drawing my power into my well as fast as possible, I evaded. "Why are you sniffing around a Vampire Compound?"

She frowned at my non-answer. "There was a dire-fire in Pacific Beach. I was sent to investigate the possibility of a rogue Coven when I sensed an incredible amount of magic." Her brows rose in inquisition. "Yours?"

Glaring, I scoffed. "You know I don't have a need for a Coven." Lifting my arm, I wiggled my fingers. "No magic, remember?"

Chuckling, she paced a line into the hardened sand. "Yes, I know." Her eyes darkened in mockery as she glanced down her nose. "Poor prodigy didn't have any power. Pathetic." Scowling, she abandoned her pacing and stalked closer to the hole in the fence. "So, Sora, whose magic—" she paused and swept her hand down the perimeter line and back "—is this, then?"

My magic soared in response to my anger. Struggling to contain it, I closed my eyes and took a deep breath. Opening them, I replied through gritted teeth, "The Clutch has their own Mage, as you well know."

Bracing her fists on her hips, she laughed. Deep peels echoed through the desert beyond. "Really?" She wiped a tear from her eye and flicked it toward the ward; it hit the invisible barrier and let out a crackle in response. She snickered and her voice took on a hard edge. "No, this is the work of a rogue Coven using Blood Magic. No single Mage"—she sneered—"especially the Clutch's wannabe, could do this."

My tone turned predatory in response to her dismissal of our Mage. Even if I hadn't met her, she was *mine*. My fangs clicked into place and I hissed, "There is no fucking Coven here."

She gasped. The snide smile slid off her face as she stepped back. "You're..." she stuttered and her face pinched in disgust. "You're one of *them*."

Offended at her accusing tone, I growled. "They are *mine*, as I am theirs." Stepping past the ward, I prowled through the fence and bumped her with my chest as Mason moved into position behind me. "My family," I hissed again, slamming her once more. "This is your one and only warning." My pupils dilated as I boomed, "LEAVE!"

Thunder and lightning rolled across the sky as the tether on my magic stretched, seeking a release for my anger.

Her face soured. Backing away, she glanced up at the impending storm.

Boom!

A strike of lightning landed just inches from where she'd been.

Glaring, she threatened, "This isn't over." Erecting a red shield of light above her head, she used magic to increase her speedy retreat.

Blaze

He paced the length of the barracks for what must have been the hundredth time since she left when thunder shook the building.

He rushed forward and gestured for someone to check the sun's descent.

Missy stepped closer and peeked out the door. Awe colored her tone. "Clouds cover the sky, Master."

He pushed open the heavy door as lightning streaked down, searing the ground where Sora had gone.

"To me!" he rumbled, flashing outside to find his Mate.

Sora

"Fuck," I whispered more to myself than Mason.

He placed a large palm on my shoulder. "Mistress?"

Disappointed in myself, I faced him.

Dropping his hand, he stood tall and proud. His lips tipped up as his brilliant blue eyes met mine. The storm let down a smattering of raindrops, wetting his severe cheeks. "You did well," he whispered. "A Council Mage would never have left otherwise."

I shook my head. "I don't think I did." Turning back to the fence, I mumbled, "She will be back though."

Blaze arrived with a contingent of our Clutch.

Mason filled him in on what happened while I wondered what to do next. Blaze barked a few orders to repair the fence before his solid chest pressed against my back. Immediately, the hard lines of my tense shoulders drooped; soothed by his proximity.

"The Council knows," I whispered, leaning against him. "What exactly, I'm not sure. They will come." My voice turned bitter as I reminisced, "Daisy never could leave well enough alone. Like a damned dog with a bone."

He rested his cheek against my temple. The silver strands of my hair whipped around us as the wind increased with my sour mood. He rumbled, "From before?"

Sheets of rain cascaded from the sky, drenching us while I tried to gather my whirlwind of thoughts. I answered in a monotone. "She was my best friend as a child. Then she received her magic and everything changed." I pinched the bridge of my nose. Goddess, what a mess.

Blaze caught a strand of hair and wrapped it around his fingers. Lightly, he tugged it to get my attention. Lowering my hand, I turned in his arms to gaze into his black eyes.

His deep bass reverberated against my chest as he swore vehemently, "Let them come."

———

Read on for an excerpt of *Allied Mage*, the second book in the Clutch Mistress Series!

Thanks for reading! If you enjoyed this book as much I have enjoyed writing it, please leave a review on Amazon.

To be notified when Janelle Peel's next book is released, follow her online at
https://m.facebook.com/clutchmistress/

VAMPIRE MAGE

Janelle Peel

ALLIED MAGE

Chapter 4
Nat

Adeep scream sounded, drawing my attention back to the circling Shifters. Dancing enthusiastically, they yipped at one another. As the mass of bodies moved, I could finally see the cause of their excitement.

Von, one of our best Trackers, lay in a limp, bloody mess on the ground. The large beasts shifted again as they attempted to find an opening to get at his prone form.

Everything slowed down.

A black shitkicker came into view and snapped out a kick at a multicolored Dingo who was boldly moving in for the kill. I focused harder and watched the thick sole connect with its massive maw, sending the Dingo tumbling backward into its brethren with brutal force. My gaze tracked a black-clad thigh and led to narrow hips.

Squinting, I tried to see more through the mass of bodies. A flash of matted blond hair, cobalt irises, and a strong jaw.

Janelle Peel

Blaze! My heart squeezed painfully in my chest.

I inhaled sharply as a rage I'd never known heated my blood. Azure flames broke along on my hands. Slowly, they trickled up my arms beneath my leather jacket.

Viv touched my shoulder.

I hissed in response.

Raising her palms, she gestured to the Mage.

I followed the motion. Yes, she was mine.

Silently, I backed out of my position and left Viv and Jackson on their own.

MINE, a growl started at the back of my throat. My flames danced higher, flickering in and out of my vision as they lit the scene around me in a blue glow.

I prowled toward the Mage with a sinister smile on my face. Thunder rolled across the sky in response to my fury.

Boom!

Her eyes opened, green in the moonlight. Silence reigned as everything quieted. Her mouth opened and closed in shock.

My hair loosened from its previous twist and snapped around my face in silver whips. Lifting an arm, I called on the storm. Lightning flashed, arcing down from the sky to my outstretched fingers. I stopped and let the bright light zip around the tips for a moment. Retribution coursed through me as I directed the bolt toward her seated form.

Find *Allied Mage* here:
https://www.amazon.com/Allied-Mage-Clutch-Mistress-Book-ebook/dp/B075FT5C7T

ALLIED MAGE

Thanks for reading! If you enjoyed this book as much I have enjoyed writing it, please leave a review on Amazon!

To be notified when Janelle Peel's next book is released, follow her online at
https://m.facebook.com/clutchmistress/

Or, sign up here to become a member of the Clutch and receive her newsletter!
http://eepurl.com/cYZlBf

Janelle Peel

More from Janelle Peel-

The Clutch Mistress Series-
Vampire Mage
Allied Mage
Chosen Mage
Alpha Mage
The Sundering
Demon's Rage

The Tabula Rasa Series-
Tidal Magic
Blood Origin
Rune Gate

The Lost Clan Chronicles-
Blood Rite

Made in the USA
Las Vegas, NV
30 January 2024